LP BECK

Beck, Harry.
A gun-handy stranger

ATCHISON PUBLIC LIBRARY
401 Kansas
Atchison, KS 66002

ATCHISON LIBRARY
401 KANSAS
ATCHISON, KS 66002

SPECIAL MESSAGE TO READERS

This book is published under the auspices of
THE ULVERSCROFT FOUNDATION
(registered charity No. 264873 UK)

Established in 1972 to provide funds for research, diagnosis and treatment of eye diseases. Examples of contributions made are: —

A new Children's Assessment Unit at Moorfield's Hospital, London.

Twin operating theatres at the Western Ophthalmic Hospital, London.

A Chair of Ophthalmology at the University of Leicester.

The establishment of a Royal Australian College of Ophthalmologists "Fellowship".

You can help further the work of the Foundation by making a donation or leaving a legacy. Every contribution, no matter how small, is received with gratitude. Please write for details to:

**THE ULVERSCROFT FOUNDATION,
The Green, Bradgate Road, Anstey,
Leicester LE7 7FU, England.
Telephone: (0116) 236 4325**

**In Australia write to:
THE ULVERSCROFT FOUNDATION,
c/o The Royal Australian College of Ophthalmologists,
27, Commonwealth Street, Sydney,
N.S.W. 2010.**

A GUN-HANDY STRANGER

Frank Zurdo wore his gun on the left side, which was unusual, but not unheard of. In Spanish his name meant 'left-handed', but all he knew about his parents was what an old woman had once told him. When Frank arrived in Heatherton, he discovered the folks there disliked the type of man he was — a rangeman. Before the smoke settled, he and the town constable had made several discoveries, and each time the discovery was accompanied by death — gunfire death.

HARRY BECK

A GUN-HANDY STRANGER

Complete and Unabridged

LINFORD
Leicester

First published in Great Britain
in 1993

London

First Linford Edition
published 1996
by arrangement with
Robert Hale Limited
London

The right of Harry Beck to be identified as
the author of this work has been asserted by
him in accordance with the
Copyright, Designs and Patents Act, 1988

Copyright © 1993 by Harry Beck
All rights reserved

British Library CIP Data

Beck, Harry
 A gun-handy stranger.—Large print ed.—
 Linford western library
 I. Title II. Series
 813.54 [F]

ISBN 0–7089–7816–9

Published by
F. A. Thorpe (Publishing) Ltd.
Anstey, Leicestershire

Set by Words & Graphics Ltd.
Anstey, Leicestershire
Printed and bound in Great Britain by
T. J. Press (Padstow) Ltd., Padstow, Cornwall

This book is printed on acid-free paper

1

Heatherton

THE wind was cold at his back, it whistled among the trees, bent saplings and made an eerie whispering sound where patches of tall, dead grass appeared in the openings on the down-slope.

His mule-nosed bay horse with the short back hiked along with his tail splayed against his flanks. He never hesitated; no horse would when he had his rump to the wind.

The sky was an unsettled, writhing dark mass. There had been no sun since the rider had picked his way over the raw granite above timberline two days earlier. Up there the wind had been fierce and fitful. Lower, it was bitingly cold but to some extent the timber broke its force.

The rider was slitty-eyed, unshaven, hunched inside his sheepskin riding coat like a turtle, only his head showed. His hat was pulled so low his eyes barely showed beneath the brim.

He'd foolishly left behind a pair of insulating hair pants — angora chaps — and as he saw open country coming up to meet the trees he wished for the hundredth time he had brought them along. The reason he'd left them hanging in someone's bunkhouse was because even when they were dry, hair pants were heavy. When they were rain-soaked it required genuine effort to walk.

They were an anachronism anyway. When he'd been young rangemen wore them; now, in his middle years, no one did, except perhaps a few die-hard old-timers. The present variety of rangemen wore split cowhide or buckskin chaps, which were much lighter and easier to move in, but they had disadvantages too.

His name was Frank Zurdo. He

was grey at the temples, his hide was weathered tan and lightly lined. His eyes were creek-gravel grey. He was medium height and muscular. He didn't look like someone with a Spanish name and maybe he wasn't. He had never known his parents. His name had been pinned on the old blanket someone had wrapped him in as a baby when they left him on a church doorstep in Kansas. He did not learn for fifteen years that in Spanish his name meant 'left handed'.

He was left handed; wore his belt-gun on the left side, rolled smokes with one hand — the left one. He roped with his left hand. An old woman back in Kansas had told him she had seen the people who abandoned him on the doorstep. She said the woman had been red-headed and the man had been sand-blond. That was all she had known.

He had left Kansas on a stolen horse when he had been young. The old woman had said he was eighteen years old.

He had done it all between his eighteenth and his forty-fourth year, and he had been very good at anything he did which included trapping wild horses which he had sold for fifty cents a head, bucked seemingly endless miles of bad weather bringing up the drag in a dozen overland cattle drives, had driven stage in Arizona Territory, had shod horses and mules for a smith in upper New Mexico and for the past three years had been top-hand for the Fleming Brothers cow outfit north of the Yellowstone.

He had almost married a lovely Crow woman seven or eight years back but her father traded her to a French trapper for seven skinny horses, three rifles and one gallon of whiskey.

When Frank Zurdo rode out after the thaw set in to see her, he was told she had left the previous winter with her Frenchman.

For the solitary rider on the downslope

toward open country with the wind against his back, life had been both good and bad. It had started out bad, but it had got better. To a man accustomed to surviving on bare bones and irregular meals, little money and much hard labour, owning a good horse, a scarred but strong Miles City saddle, two reliable weapons and freedom, the world was not a bad place. Most of the time anyway.

But Frank Zurdo was neither a laughing nor talkative individual. He had learned early that in this world there are only two kinds of people, the ones who were honest and the ones who weren't. He chose friends carefully, had never partnered with anyone but was not quite a loner. If he had been he would not have aimed for the distant rooftops of the town he saw southeasterly as he rode clear of the uplands and their timber-screen.

He did not reach the town; he probably could have but his horse was tired and Frank was hungry. They dry-camped in an arroyo where only occasional flurries of wind reached.

In the morning they struck out with the same lowering menace of black clouds overhead but the wind had blown itself out, which was a blessing. Of all nature's elements Frank had encountered he disliked wind the most. A man could get warm with a little fire, he could find a creek to cool off in, but there was no way to find relief from a hard wind.

The town looked ragged and cowed when he entered from the north. There were no horses at the tie-racks and hardly any people about. It was too early for the place to show much life but Frank did not own a watch and there was no sun to gauge the hours by. It was shortly after five in the morning when he swung off in the livery barn doorway and led his horse inside. The town's name was Heatherton, changed only recently from what its earlier inhabitants had called it — Nowhere — someone's whimsical irony, because for a fact there was nothing but open rolling country in all directions, few trees, just miles of grass that tipped and swayed in the wind like ocean waves.

It was dismal-dark from one end of Heatherton to the other end. It was especially dark in the livery barn runway where someone was approaching in an old blanket-coat and pants stuffed inside coarse cowhide boots. If there had been a hat Frank would have thought the liveryman badly needed a haircut, a luxury Frank himself had been unable to get for two months.

He stepped ahead of his horse with reins extended as he started to say grain, hay, a decent cuffing and a dry stall, when the words dried up. The figure in the old blanket-coat was a woman.

Frank had encountered women in lots of places, but never running a livery business before. He had even once known a woman called Hardy who was a blacksmith who had biceps like a quarter horse, chewed tobacco and could make a man's hair stand straight up when she swore.

But this woman was not as broad as Hardy had been; she was definitely feminine, and she was pretty. Tired-looking, dressed in faded britches, wearing ancient boots with the inevitable detritus that went with liverying — manured boots. She took his reins as he found his tongue.

"Grain, ma'm, a clean stall, plenty of hay and clean water."

She nodded. Even in poor light he thought her eyes were as blue as cornflowers. The only words she spoke were: "For how long?"

Frank had no idea. "A few days maybe. Long enough to get shaved and washed an' fed good. Is there a boarding house?"

She was turning away when she gestured northward with her hand. Frank watched for a moment wondering what in the hell a woman was doing working as a hostler in someone's livery barn.

The boarding house was a ramshackle building, half old peeled logs, half planed wood. The proprietor was a tall, rawboned old man with an eagle's beak and eyes that were flat and expressionless. He took Frank's two-bits, led him down a dingy hall where one smoky coal oil lamp hung, halted in front of a door and jerked his head. Not a word passed between them as Frank opened the door, closed it, dumped his saddlebags and booted Winchester, tested the bed, which had rope springs, swung his arms to stir circulation, pulled up a chair, shed his boots, his hat and gun belt, sat down facing southward down through Heatherton satisfied that it being early and all, the hotelman and the liverylady probably hadn't had their coffee yet, otherwise they wouldn't have been so short.

The sun did not come but Heatherton came grudgingly to life. As Frank went in search of the cafe he did not see a single smiling face. Well hell, dismal weather affected folks like that, including Frank Zurdo.

The cafeman was also curt and unsmiling. Frank was his first patron. He brought hot coffee first, which was customary, retreated into his cooking area and went noisily to work back there.

Two townsmen came in. One was short with rosy cheeks and black cotton sleeve protectors from the cuff to his elbows. He would be a merchant, no one else wore those things. The second man was nondescript with a coffee-stained downward drooping dragoon mustache, little pale eyes and a large nose made more noticeable by the cold morning which coloured it red.

They both nodded to Frank, went to the lower end of the counter, hunkered down there like buzzards on a tree limb. When the cafeman came they growled their orders. He growled back, brought their coffee and said, "Well, gawddammit, what did you expect?"

Neither man replied, they became

occupied with their coffee. Frank's meal came, floating in grease and smelling like pure ambrosia to someone who'd been living off the land.

Dawn did not truly arrive but the world had to brighten; it was morning, the world always brightened when a new day arrived.

Frank found the tonsorial parlour, was shaved and shorn by a man who looked like he'd been sucking lemons, and who, contrary to traditional and perhaps historic custom, did not say a word until Frank had been made presentable and asked for soap, a towel and the key to the wash house out back.

The barber held out his paw. "Ten cents," he said, and did not move until he had the coin, then he rummaged for a chunk of brown soap and a clean towel. The last thing he handed over was the key. This time he spoke. "Damned rats been pluggin' the drain hole. You'll see a long stick leanin' against the wall. I'd take it kindly if you'd run that stick through the drain pipe before you pull the plug."

It took a while to get the water hot; there was no kindling. Frank had to hunt for dry wood outside. By the time the fire-box's load of water was heated he was beginning to wonder if the people he'd met so far in Heatherton had been beaten with a mean-stick when they'd been born, or if something had happened in the town that had upset the hell out of them.

He had visited lots of range towns — and villages — in his time; mostly they'd had two kinds of inhabitants, nasty ones and nice ones. Heatherton seemed to be where only unpleasant ones lived.

He did not intend to stay much past the time it took to get the pleats out of his stomach, the grime off his carcass, and sleep up off the ground for a night or two.

There was a saloon in town on the east side between a mercantile store and a little hole in the wall shop owned and operated by a seamstress, a widow-woman in her fifties named Alicia Hovencroft.

Frank had never been much of a drinker, even in cold weather when whiskey was supposed to warm a man's cockles, of which Frank had no idea about and had never asked.

He liked beer in summer, but only one glass, the second ones did not taste as good as the first, and a third glass did not taste good at all.

He soaked, relaxed, thought back to the far side of those hostile granite jags he had crossed to get down here, switched to other, more pleasant reflections and finally climbed out of the tin tub, toweled off and got dressed. When he opened the door to depart a wizened old man with eyes like a ferret arose from a stump and caustically said, "If I'd known you was goin' to be in there so long I'd have stuck a clutch of eggs under you."

Frank had been fed, shaved, bathed and rested. He was by most standards a patient man, but the most patient of men, someone named Job, had a limit. Frank closed the bath-house door and leaned on it. The old man reddened, he cleared his gullet, spat aside and was about to make another sour remark when Frank reached without haste, got a handful of the old gaffer's shirt, pulled him in close and said, "What the hell's wrong with this town? First, I got cut off by a female at the livery barn, then the old scarecrow who runs the roomin' house, then by the cafeman, the barber, an' now you, an' for a damned fact I've never seen any of you before . . . Are you folks just naturally nasty?"

The old man squirmed to free himself. Frank released his grip. The old man was still red in the face as he shoved his shirttail in and glowered. "We don't like strangers," he snarled. "Specially rangemen."

"Is that a fact? You folks got a reason or are you just naturally cranky?"

The old man was holding a threadbare

towel and a piece of soap in one hand, which hindered the tucking-in process. He said, "We got a reason. A damned good reason. Now get out of my way or you'll be carryin' your guts in a bucket."

The old man held a skinning knife in his free hand. Frank had neither seen the knife or the old man draw it nor had expected him to. The old man was not wearing a gun and shell-belt.

Frank softly wagged his head and moved clear of the door. He returned to the barber's place, tossed his soggy towel with the bar of soap on the cutting chair and was starting to ask who that disagreeable old bastard was out back when the barber jumped over, grabbed the wet towel off his chair and snarled. "You raised in a barn, mister?"

Frank walked out into the gloomy, overcast day, thought there was the smell of rain in the air and walked across the road heading southward in the direction of the livery barn.

Born horsemen never neglected to make certain their livestock was well cared for.

A little ankle-high wind was gusting, raising dust out front. Inside, the dark runway had been raked clean. The wind did not come inside otherwise there would have been more dust, this time with a different scent.

His horse was full as a tick, sound asleep with one hind leg cocked, his lower lip drooping. There was still some sweet timothy hay in the corner manger and a full bucket of water against the wall.

Satisfied, he was turning when he heard someone sobbing. It sounded like a child. The noise was barely louder than scrabbling gusts of roadway wind. It seemed to be coming from the harness room.

2

Getting Acquainted

FRANK'S knowledge of women was limited. He hadn't reached his present age without encountering his share of them, but he'd only had one love in his life and only God knew where she was, with her damned Frenchman.

He stood in the harness-room door solemnly considering the auburn-haired woman in the old blanket coat with her face hidden by both arms sitting at a rickety wooden desk. He had seen women cry before; it made him uncomfortable. He stood in the doorway thinking this was none of his business. Another thought occurred: This damned town . . .

The liverylady looked up, saw Frank and made several quick swipes with a woolen sleeve to dry her face as she asked in a mechanical voice if he wanted his horse.

Frank entered the little gloomy room, sat on an up-turned horseshoe keg, leaned looking at her and asked a question. "Did somethin' happen in this town, ma'm? Everyone I've come onto either won't talk or acts mean."

The pretty woman with eyes the colour of corn flowers, lustily blew her nose, pocketed the handkerchief and considered Frank before speaking. "Me'n my husband bought this business from an old man two years back. Clary was a born horseman; we built up this business, even got two light freight rigs. We traded around. In two years we did right well . . ."

The tears welled up. The liverylady turned her head, pulled down a ragged big breath, held it briefly and expelled it. She turned back. "Clary was not a drinking man . . . We married over in Missouri six years back . . . Mister, it was hard until we got this business. We was going to make it . . . "

Frank rolled a one-handed smoke and lighted it in order to give her time to stifle the sobs. As he removed it from his mouth she said, "He wasn't a drinkin' man. He went up to the saloon because Mister Bolton has the only safe in town. He wanted to put some money in Mister Bolton's safe . . . He was killed up there . . . Clary wasn't armed. He owned a gun, two guns, but he didn't wear a gun."

Frank considered cigarette ash, tipped it off, smoked for another moment then killed the cigarette and pitched it out into the runway. Her husband must have been liked, if his killing was what had everyone so sour and disagreeable. Or maybe it was an unarmed man getting shot; that would not set well in most places.

He didn't know what to say so he said nothing. Outside that ankle-high autumn wind was still gusting. Loose boards slapped, dust sifted. Frank arose, nodded and walked out into the runway. Two rangemen riding side by side passed northward from the lower end of town.

Frank went up to the saloon where two tail-tucked horses stood patiently at the tie-rack. There were four customers, the two rangemen Frank had seen from the livery barn runway, and two old men sitting close to the big canon heater where wood had been stacked against the wall.

The saloonman was a moon-faced individual with a wound for a mouth, hard, cynical eyes and a respectable paunch. Frank nodded for beer and watched the saloonman pump a glass full. Farther up the bar the pair of rangemen were eyeing Frank with clear interest. When the beer came Frank half-emptied the glass and rolled another one-handed smoke. Not everyone could do that. The rangemen watched and one laughed as he shook his head. "I must've spilt a hunnert pounds of tobacco tryin' to do that."

They weren't young men, possibly in

their late twenties or maybe their early thirties, but they had the lined faces of older men. Lifetimes spent out of doors did that.

Frank offered to stand them some beer, which completely broke the ice. They accepted, the cold-eyed saloonman set them up. The rangeman who had laughed said, "I'm Jim Flood, this here is Ralph Turner. We call him Centre Fire. He rides a centre fire saddle."

Frank smiled a little and nodded. "Frank Zurdo."

"You on your way south?"

Frank shrugged. "On my way anywhere it don't snow three feet every winter."

"From where?"

"Montana."

The genial rider dryly said, "Frank, you better hustle; it snows that much in Colorado an' it's late in the year."

The other man had sunk-set, thoughtful eyes. Somewhere he had acquired a broken nose which had healed slightly to the right of where it should have been. He was the man introduced as Ralph Turner — Centre Fire. He emptied his glass, pushed it aside and spoke with a faint Texas accent. "If the weather holds, Frank, you could maybe make it down to New Messico. But you got to go dang near to the Mex border before it don't snow."

Frank nodded. He knew all these things. "You boys hired on permanent?"

The genial man, Jim Flood, leaned sideways along the bar, standing loose. "We been kept on for three years to feed for an old man name of Hart Thomas. He goes down to Denver every winter. He says the cold bothers his old bones."

Frank knew about that too. Several big outfits he had worked for were left in the hands of hired men to winter feed while owners went where it was warmer. The pay was better and the work was harder. He had winter-fed for the last two outfits he had worked for, and this was what had finally decided him to go back south.

The moon-faced barman had dusted his backbar during this exchange. He only turned when Ralph Turner offered to pay for the next round. He refilled the glasses without speaking and with his expression the same — blank as a stone wall. Turner paid for the beers, looked at the saloonman thoughtfully and said, "Henry, them things happen."

The saloonman looked steadily at the rangeman. Frank thought he was going to speak but he didn't, he turned his back and went back to dusting his back-bar.

Turner reddened, his sunk-set gaze on the older man's back was cold. Evidently Jim Flood knew his companion fairly well because he spoke quickly. "It's time to pick up the mail an' head back." Flood stepped away from the bar. Turner also stepped back, but slowly; Frank thought reluctantly. He made a mental note about Centre-Fire

Turner; he was a touchy individual.

After the riders had departed Frank leaned on the bar watching the back-bar get dusted before he quietly asked a question. "What was Clary's last name?"

The saloonman turned. "Devon. Clary Devon," he replied, looking as steadily at Frank as he had looked at Ralph Turner.

Frank returned the gaze. "You'd be Mister Bolton?"

"Henry Bolton. And you?"

"Frank Zurdo."

Bolton loosened lightly. "You Mex, Mister Zurdo?"

"No. Not that I know of. Why?"

"Do you speak Mex?"

"No. I have a hard enough time with English."

Bolton relaxed a little more. "Zurdo in Spanish or Mex means left-handed."

Frank nodded. "So I've been told."

Bolton leaned over the bar, straightened back and said, "You're left-handed?"

"Yep. Born that way I guess."

Bolton studied Frank for a moment before speaking again. "A man wears his gun on the left side an' don't speak Mex whose name is Zurdo . . . Unusual, Mister Zurdo."

Frank's slatey gaze neither wavered nor blinked. "Why do I get the feelin', Mister Bolton, that you think I'm an outlaw?"

Henry Bolton's gaze slid away and returned. "I've been in this business a long time, Mister Zurdo. It gets to be sort of second nature to speculate about customers. No offense, Mister Zurdo."

"Frank. Just plain Frank."

Bolton sounded relieved when he replied. "Henry. My paw was Mister Bolton."

Frank smiled. "Buy you a drink, Henry?"

"One. I sell it I don't drink it. Whiskey all right?"

"Only beer," Frank replied, and watched the saloonman get their drinks and return. He seemed less testy as he saluted and downed his straight jolt. Frank tasted his beer before putting it aside to lean more comfortably as he asked another question.

"Everywhere I've been in Heatherton folks are cranky. Before I came up here I walked in on the lady down at the livery barn settin' in the dark crying. Just now I got the feelin' you didn't feel real friendly with those two rangemen."

Henry Bolton leaned against his back-bar with folded arms before saying, "Do you ride for anyone around here?"

"Henry; you heard what I told those cowboys. I've never been in the Heatherton country before in my life an' I don't know any stockmen nor work for them."

"Her name's Elizabeth. Her husband an' most folks around town call her Buffy . . . They come here a few years back. He ferriered until they saved enough to buy the livery business . . . Ten days ago her husband come up here of a Saturday night to store some money in my safe. Those two who was just in here, Turner and Flood, was here too, that night. A mean-tempered rider named Sage Beaman had been drinkin' steady. Folks give him a wide berth. He's got a bad reputation. I was tryin' to figure a way to get him out of the saloon when young Clary Devon come in. I didn't see it happen, all I heard was Sage swearin' loud, then a gunshot. Afterwards Sage was goin' out the door with the rest of us froze, when he said, 'That'll teach the son of a bitch not to jostle folks at the bar.'"

Frank considered his beer, decided not to and asked if folks in Heatherton had liked Clary Devon. The saloonman nodded. "He was young, friendly as a pup, worked hard, never strayed . . . I'd say you'd have to look hard to find someone who didn't like him."

Frank said, "Well, that explains why everyone was so disagreeable when I rode in."

"Mister, you're a rangeman," Bolton

replied. "But Clary wasn't armed. That makes it murder. I've never been any place where folks took kindly to murder, have you?"

"No."

"It's one of them things that sticks in folk's craw. Some of the outlyin' cow outfits, so I've heard, have told their riders to stay out of town for a while."

"Care for another jolt on me, Henry?"

"No thanks. I don't use the stuff very often. Like I said, I sell it but don't drink it . . . Often anyway."

"You mentioned folks not likin' murder, I've been where they've hanged fellers. That struck me as some sort of murder."

The barman went after a high stool and perched on it before resuming their discussion. His legs had been troubling him lately. Standing up for sometimes as many as five, six hours every night except Sunday was hard on the feet and legs. Particularly so if a man was, like

Henry Bolton, sturdily overweight.

"I'll tell you a little story, Frank. Once, back in Ohio I pulled on a hang-rope behind an old feller who was the local preacher. He grunted right along with the rest of us. It bothered me, so the following winter I asked him how he came to do that, an' what he said stuck in my mind. He said men made the law an' God made us know the difference between man-made law and God's justice. Does that sound right to you?"

Frank showed one of his rare smiles. "Sounds real good to me . . . Henry, how long is this bad feelin' goin' to last, because if I know rangemen, an' I'd ought to know 'em I been one most of my life, no matter who tells 'em not to come to town, they'll come, an' if it's a challenge they'll come loaded for bear."

Bolton nodded. "Folks understand that. If they come ruttin' folks will be ready."

Frank sighed, considered his beer and

reached for the glass. It wouldn't be the first time townsmen and rangemen tangled horns. As he put the empty glass aside and turned his head to discreetly belch, Henry Bolton said, "I know. One killin' can start a massacre."

Frank rolled another one-handed quirley and lit it. "Don't seem to me the rangemen an' the townsmen should go to war because one feller murdered another feller."

"But they will. There's never been a lot of good-feelin' between the two, and this time the fuse is lit. I got no idea how to stop it."

"Get hold of Sage Beaman. Settle with him."

Henry Bolton sighed. "He hasn't been back since the killing, an' when he sobered up I expect he knew the best thing for him to do is not come back. Maybe never."

Frank looked around as several customers arrived. He recognised only two of them, the storekeeper with the cotton sleeve-protectors and the tall, lean man who had been with him down at the cafe.

Henry went to look after the new arrivals. Frank put several coins beside his empty glass and returned to the roadway. The day was dying, which surprised him. He had no idea he'd spent that much time with the saloonman.

Down at the cafe the place was crowded. The cafeman passed Frank a curt nod. He was busier than a horse in fly-time.

The scarecrow who owned the boarding house was at the counter. He and Frank exchanged a nod. When the scarecrow's wife had been alive room-and-board was the way the place had been run, but after her passing although it was still called a boarding house, it was actually a roominghouse.

Frank saw faces he had seen before. When his meal arrived he enjoyed it as he had before. Almost anything beat eating out of a dented fry-pan over smoking little fires.

He went out front, had a smoke, saw the lady liveryman climb on a chair out front to light the pair of carriage lamps, climb down and drag the chair along as she went back down the runway.

He killed his smoke and walked down there. One thing had bothered him today. Although there was a log jailhouse almost opposite the cafe, it was not lighted and for a fact had the desolate appearance of a building no one worked in.

There had to be a lawman. Heatherton was not a village. Henry Bolton had not mentioned a lawman. As he reached the front entrance of the livery barn the blue-eyed widow appeared. They exchanged a look before she said, "I like the evenings. I like the smell of the night air, the stars, the moon when it's up there."

Frank nodded, passed to an old bench and sat down. He liked evenings too; in fact, except for wind, he liked everything out of doors. He said,

"Bother you if I smoke?"

She looked around at him, surprised. She could not recall anyone asking her that before, men just naturally lighted up.

"No, I don't mind, mister . . . ?"

"Zurdo. Frank Zurdo. Frank would be fine. Your name is Elizabeth, isn't it?"

"Yes. But I haven't been called that since I was a child. I'm Buffy Devon."

She watched fascinated as Frank rolled his one-handed quirley.

There were plenty of stars, it was a clear night, but the moon was little more than a lop-sided slice off something pale and distant.

3

A Pleasant Day — Almost

THE following day he was down at the livery barn. He had taken his horse out of the stall; confined horses had a way of stocking up. Sometimes they got colic.

He was leaning out back watching his horse roll forth and back. Among horsemen there was a saying that for every time a horse could roll completely over and back he was worth ten dollars. Frank's did it three times before jumping up wide-legged to shake like a dog coming out of a creek.

There was no wind, the sky was flawless blue, the sun was up there bright as it could be without sending off very much heat this time of year.

He heard the man in the runway

say, "Lady, I never pay more'n two bits for stallin' cuffin' an' feedin' my horse."

Frank straightened up, but whatever Buffy Devon replied he could not make out. The man spoke again, his words carrying well as he said, "Do it lady; cuff him off, feed him real good, when I come back I'll look in to make sure you done it."

Frank sighed, strolled around the side of the barn from out back and stood in the doorway. Buffy and the big, unshaven man were mid-way along. They saw him. The man ignored Frank, shoved his reins into the woman's hand and growled as he was turning to depart. "Two bits is more'n it's worth. Fifteen cents is plenty. I'll be back."

Frank scarcely raised his voice. "Two bits, friend. In advance."

The unshaven man turned back. "Are you the liveryman?"

"No, I'm just passing through. Give her two bits, friend."

The stranger hooked both thumbs in his shellbelt as he silently regarded Frank. You got a horse here?" he asked.

Frank nodded. Yeah, an' I paid two bits."

"I never paid more'n fifteen cents."

"Maybe not, friend, but two bits is the lady's charge."

The large man said, "You don't want trouble with me, cowboy."

Frank's reply was quietly given. "You're right, I don't, but unless you give her what she charges, I'm going to, friend."

The large man shifted stance, looked from Frank to the woman, fished in a pocket, handed Buffy a quarter of a dollar, turned on his heel and stamped up to the roadway.

Frank walked up the runway. "I was wonderin'," he said, "if he'd have argued if you had been a man."

Buffy looked steadily at Frank. "I carry a derringer, Mister Zurdo."

He smiled slightly. "I didn't know

that. You can leave my horse out back if you're of a mind to. He needs to move around."

"Are you leaving soon, Mister Zurdo?"

"Frank, I told you. Just plain Frank ... I don't know. But I'll have to make up my mind soon. They tell me it snows hard around here an' that's why I was headin' south. I've had about all the cold winters and tall snowbanks I need."

"I guess I'll have to keep looking then," she said.

"Looking for what?"

"A hostler."

Frank hadn't anticipated this. He hadn't worked in a livery barn since he'd dunged out for an old crank back in Missouri. "You can find someone," he told her, and walked up to the front roadway heading for the cafe.

The cafeman was civil for a change. He served Frank's meal as he said, "Nice day. It'd suit me fine if it stayed like this all winter."

There were several other diners at the

counter. Frank did not recognise but one man, the big, unshaven, dark-eyed man from the livery barn.

They exchanged an unwavering stare which the cafeman interrupted when he went down to re-fill the stranger's coffee cup.

Frank used bread to swab his plate clean, put silver on the counter, arose and walked outside to roll a smoke. That storekeeper with the sleeve protectors passed and nodded. It never took long in a place no larger than Heatherton for people to nod at strangers who had been in town for a few days.

A tired-looking old stage coach with peeling paint and a body loose enough for the doors to rattle passed by. The whip nodded, Frank nodded back. The coach went up to the north end of town and turned in where two wide wooden gates sagged as though they hadn't been closed in years.

Frank ground his smoke underfoot as someone spoke in a growly voice behind him. He turned, it was the dark-eyed villainous looking individual from the livery barn. He had said, "I'm fifty. By the time a man gets that age he figures things — like killin' you down yonder over two bits. It ain't worth it, not for no two bits."

"It wasn't the two bits," Frank replied. "It was you bullyin' the widow woman."

"I wasn't bullyin' her. Hell, every place I been the last few years they charge fifteen cents."

"Well, it's her barn. She can charge what she wants." Frank shoved out a hand. "Frank Zurdo."

The big man regarded the hand briefly then gripped it and smiled. "Fred Baca. Who's head In'ian in Heatherton?"

Frank had no idea. "Ask over at the general store. I only been here a couple of days."

He watched the large man cross to the store. There was something . . .

Frank went up the east side plankwalk

and encountered that turkey-necked stringbean who had been with the storekeeper at the cafe. The tall man was sitting on a bench out front of a saddle and harness works. They exchanged a nod before the tall older man said, "It's the wrong time of the year to get hired on."

Frank stopped. "I'm not lookin' for any winter-feedin' job. I'm on my way south so's I won't have to stand in snow up to my belt."

The tall old man had a hawk nose and shrewd small faded blue eyes. "Is that a fact? I wondered. I saw you down at the livery barn a couple of times."

"I got my horse down there," Frank said, sitting down on the same old bench. "He needs gettin' fed up an' rested."

The old man seemed not to have heard. "She's mighty pretty, for a fact. An' no doubt about it, she needs another man . . . On top of that the barn's a good business."

Frank stared.

The old man leaned as though to arise. "I got hot coffee inside if you're of a mind," he said, arose and entered the leather works without glancing back to see if Frank had followed.

He had. The tall man drew off two tin cups full from a small, popping iron stove. As he went behind the counter he said, "A man could do a lot worse. Rangeridin's fine when you're young an' dumb, but when a man gets a tad of grey around the ears he'd do better than to go no farther than the first opportunity."

Frank didn't know what to say so he leaned, waiting for the black java to cool.

You'll be Frank Zurdo," the old man said, leaning against his cutting table. "I'm Wesly Hamilton."

Frank nodded, the tall man nodded back and spoke again, "Finish your coffee, Frank. I got to go down to the general store. They're havin' a meetin' down there about a feller name of Baca who answered one of our letters for a town marshal."

Frank finished his coffee but did not straighten up off the counter immediately. "I met him a while back."

"Baca?"

Yes. Big feller with dark eyes. I'd say he could handle whatever he had to — if he had to."

"Is he a Mex?"

"I don't know. If he is, he's not a very dark one." Frank put the cup aside and pulled back off the counter. "What happened to your last town marshal?"

"He upped and quit. He showed me a letter from an old friend out in Californie. It said there was gold all over out there. I don't believe it, but you can't blame a man for wantin' to get rich."

Frank went out front, waited until the tall old man locked up, then watched him cross over walking in the direction of the general store.

The bench was where sunshine

struck. It was a pleasant place to loaf. Frank rolled a smoke and lighted up. A tall woman whose handsomeness was fading, crossed the road and entered a small store which had a sign in the window: Alicia Hovencroft, Seamstress.

He was becoming capable of placing people. Names didn't much matter, faces did. He watched a battered old wagon with sideboards enter town from the northeast. It parked out front of the general store, a man climbed down, made his hitch fast and beat off dust before entering the store. There was a burnt brand on the side of the wagon below the seat but it was too distant for Frank to make it out.

He crossed over to the saloon where a fuzz-faced young man was minding the bar. He volunteered the information that Mister Bolton was down at the general store for some kind of town meeting.

Frank took his beer to a table, sat facing the roadway and placed both booted feet on a chair. Evidently Heatherton had a town council, which was about right; it wasn't large enough to have a mayor along with a council.

He was becoming more familiar with the town and its inhabitants by the day. But it was time to ride south. He'd only intended to lie over for a couple of days, until both he and his horse rested up from crossing those granite peaks above timberline that looked to be maybe thirty miles from town, but the air was glass-clear, which made distances deceptive.

The fuzz-faced youth brought Frank an old newspaper. The price of beef was up in Omaha — two dollars a head. The military was having trouble with Indians down in Arizona Territory, which was nothing new, and some man whose picture made him look bald as a badger and heavy through the body was proclaiming his willingness to serve the people and the nation when the next presidential election rolled around.

The newspaper was two months old

and was limp from passing through many hands. Frank put it atop the table. There was nothing in it that would interest readers in an isolated place like Heatherton.

A rangeman came in without bothering to knock off dust. Frank recognised him; it was the man named Turner who was called Centre Fire.

The fuzz-faced youth served Turner, who turned, saw Frank, and walked over holding his full little jolt glass.

Frank nodded and gestured. "Set."

The man with sunk-set eyes sat, tipped his head, dropped the contents of his little glass straight down, put the glass aside, leaned on the table and exhaled a flammable breath before speaking. "Kind of figured you'd be gone ... Snow could come any time now. Heatherton gets snow-bound every few years, an' it gets cold. Real cold."

Frank replied casually. "In a day or two. I know snow can come. I'm rested up and been fed good. My horse is ready. Maybe tomorrow . . . Buy you another drink?"

"No thanks, I just drove in for supplies. I'll be headin' back before I get caught in the dark."

After the man referred to as Centre Fire was gone, Frank idly speculated; in the Southwest men rode centre fire saddles. He'd never seen one up in Montana, and on his way south he hadn't seen a saddle rigged centre fire either. Ralph Turner must be a Southwesterner.

He took the newspaper and his empty glass to the bar, left them atop it, put a coin beside the glass and returned to the roadway.

The meeting in the back room of the general store must have broken up, the harness-shop man along with Henry Bolton and several others were emerging from the store. One of those men had something shiny on his coat. Fred Baca had been hired as the new town marshal.

Frank went down to the livery barn.

Buffy Devon had a fire in the harness-room stove. She looked up when he appeared in the doorway. She still looked wan but her small smile was pleasant as he came in and perched on the upturned horseshoe keg as he said, "The feller you argued with about how much you charged? He's just been hired on as the town marshal."

She replied tartly. "I hope he keeps his horse in the shed behind the jailhouse . . . Mister Zurdo?"

He sighed. "Frank, ma'm. Just Frank."

"Frank; you wouldn't re-consider?"

He shook his head. "I'm leaving directly, besides with winter comin' on there'll be riders out of work. You could get the saloonman to keep his eyes open for someone."

"Do you know anything about doctoring livestock?" she asked.

Frank shrugged. "Some. I've had to do it a few times. Why?"

"My favourite horse, a chestnut mare my husband gave me last

Christmas . . . I think she has a bone felon."

Frank stood up. "That's pretty simple. Where is she?"

The mare was in a stall where shadows lingered. She had nice eyes, a good head and was in good flesh. Before the woman opened the door Frank leaned. The mare was not favouring, she had all four feet under her.

When they entered the stall the mare nuzzled Frank. He knew her kind, gentle, tractable, maybe with some minor quirk but in general thoroughly trustworthy. He ran his hand down her back so she would know where he was, over her rump and lifted a hind foot. Buffy Devon leaned close to point. "There, in the hock."

Frank put the leg down, felt the swelling, found no hardness and speculated about it being a through pin. If it was there was no cure. But where there should have been hardness the flesh was soft. It was slightly warm, though.

He led the mare out where the light was better, stood a while looking, then said, "If you got a lantern we could use it."

As soon as the woman was gone Frank took out his clasp knife, leaned, felt for the softest spot, pinched the hot skin and slashed it. The mare jumped and snorted.

When Buffy returned with the lighted lamp she held it up and gasped. Frank pocketed his knife. "Pus, ma'm. She had a fairsized sliver. Let it drain. Lucky for her it's not fly time. Keep it clean. It'll heal in time."

He put the mare back in her stall and wondered for the hundredth time why women preferred mares to geldings. He never would find the answer.

They returned to the harness room. Buffy placed the lamp overhead and sat at the old desk. "I'll pay twice hostler wages, Frank."

He smiled at her. "That's decent of you, but my horse don't like snow any better'n I do."

He left her, went up to the cafe, found a place between the storekeeper with the sleeve protectors and the stringbean who ran the leather works. The tall old man introduced them. "This here is Frank Zurdo. Frank, this here is Everett Lewis, he owns the emporium." Frank and the pudgy, smiling man shook hands as the cafeman came along. They gave their orders, the cafeman got their coffee, and Wesly Hamilton was raising his cup as he said, "You read him about right, Frank. We hired him." The storekeeper nodded vigorously. "He had the best qualifications of anyone who seemed interested. Deputy sheriff down in Texas, U.S. Marshal for In'ian Territory, Constable of Kileen on the south desert."

Frank sat perfectly still for a moment. That was what had bothered him. Kileen in southern New Mexico. He'd never met Fred Baca down there but he'd heard quite a bit about him. He was a mountain lion when he got upset.

He was experienced with his fists and deadly fast with a six-gun.

He ate in silence. When the other men were ready to leave Frank had a third cup of coffee. Now Baca's crankiness at the livery barn fitted; Baca was a quick-tempered man who took offense easily.

Frank finished at the cafe, strolled up to the saloon where smoke lay in layers about head-high, and noisy men were strung along the bar, with a few having spilled over to the poker tables.

He recognised some, nodded to those he did not know but who nodded to him. There were four or five rangemen, the others were clearly residents of the town.

Henry Bolton winked as he sailed past with four beer glasses in his hands. On the way back he hesitated long enough to say, "We finally got a town marshal." Someone was boisterously banging a glass atop the bar, Henry left Frank in a hurry.

He drank his beer thoughtfully. What

he had heard about Fred Baca was not necessarily bad, but it seemed that Heatherton most likely did not need a lawman who would attack at the drop of a hat.

From what he had been told at the cafe, it appeared Fred Baca had held a fair amount of jobs. Ordinarily lawmen did not move from job to job that often.

Frank finished his beer, went out into the settling night, studied the stars, remembered what Buffy Devon had said, and went hiking in the direction of the boarding house.

4

The Inevitable

EVEN in a detached way when a man decides his personal conviction regarding right and wrong has been violated he is likely to be sensitive to challenges, which was what encouraged the dispute in Henry Bolton's establishment the evening following Frank's polite refusal of Buffy Devon's offer.

Slightly less than a month had passed since the killing of Buffy Devon's husband. The community was still incensed, but less so than it had been immediately after the killing. Even the most sullenly resentful people lose impetus. Fortunately for humankind the bad things in life may never be forgotten, but their impetus fades with time, which could have been responsible for the arrival in Henry's saloon of several rangemen among whom was the killer of Buffy Devon's husband.

Sage Beaman was a large man, powerfully put together. He was in essence a bully, but demonstrated this less when sober than when he had been drinking.

When Beaman and his friends arrived, Henry started to sweat. It was a little early for his regulars from around town to show up but what worried him was what would happen when they walked in and saw the man they thoroughly disliked drinking with his range-rider companions.

Frank Zurdo was already at the bar with a half-empty glass of beer when the cowmen walked in. He could tell from Henry's apprehensive expression that something was suddenly different.

Ralph Turner — Centre Fire — was with the stockmen. He nodded at Frank. The last rangeman to enter was Centre Fire's friend, Jim Flood.

He and Frank also exchanged nods.

Bolton set them up for the rangemen, who occupied the uppermost end of Henry's bar.

Frank noticed the big dark-eyed man with not the faintest idea of who he was, except that he clearly dominated his companions. When he spoke the others either agreed or laughed when they were supposed to.

Frank felt mildly antagonistic; like most men he could recognise a big, blustery bully when he saw one. But he sipped his beer; most places a man went he ran into at least one like that large rangeman. He had also encountered the clutch of sycophants who invariably gathered around such men.

Townsmen began arriving. Once, as Henry hurried past, he looked at Frank and rolled his eyes heavenward. Henry was upset.

Frank finished his beer, felt the rising tension and turned slightly to look around the room. The latest patrons of Henry's place said very little among themselves and wore an identical expression of disapproval.

Frank knew of the ill-will between townsmen and rangemen after the killing. He decided to go outside for a breath of fresh night air. As he was placing the coin beside his empty glass the spindle doors swung wide and noisily closed after the last arrival. As Frank turned he froze. Fred Baca the new marshal was standing stock-still in the middle of the room looking challengingly at the rangemen. For Frank, it was too late to make a leisurely departure, the atmosphere in Henry's saloon was such that to draw attention to oneself by moving when no one else was moving, could cause trouble, so Frank turned back, snagged Henry's attention and nodded for a re-fill. When Henry returned with the full glass he leaned to whisper, "If you're a prayin' man, now'd be a good time. You see that big noisy feller? That's Sage Beaman, the one shot Clary Devon in here a few weeks back."

Henry hurried to care for a rangeman who was banging the bartop with his little jolt glass. Henry set up a fresh bottle.

Frank set his back to the bar eyeing the marshal. If all he'd heard about Fred Baca was just half true, he was about to witness real trouble.

Baca remained in the centre of the room as he said, "Which one of you gents is Sage Beaman?"

There was not a sound as the large rangeman turned to face the other large man. "I am."

Baca surprised Frank. He did not raise his voice when he said, "Mister Beaman, there's a lot of bad feeling in town. I don't want no trouble. I'm the new town marshal. I'd take it right kindly if you'd walk out of here an' don't come back."

Frank let his breath out very slowly as the dark-eyed stockman made a thin, humourless small smile. He copied the quiet tone of the marshal when he said, "I didn't catch your name."

"Fred Baca."

"Mister Baca, you bein' new in the country I'll give you some advice. This here is mostly cow country. Stockmen got every right to come an' go as they like." Beaman's smile faded, his dark eyes glowed.

Frank was startled by the sharp interruption when Centre Fire addressed the saloonman. "Henry, put both your hands atop the bar." It was common knowledge that the saloonman kept two weapons on a shelf below his bar, an ash spoke to break up fist fights, and a sawed off shotgun. Henry raised both hands to the top of his bar.

The two large men had not looked away from each other. Beaman said, "Marshal, don't start nothin', you're out-numbered five to one."

To Frank Zurdo the expression on the marshal's face supported what he had heard of the man. "You're goin' to leave town," he said, still in that almost-mild tone. "One way or the other."

Sage Beaman had been slouching against the bar. Now, he eased upright very slowly. "You'll be a fool if you try it," he replied.

Frank also straightened up. Henry was standing like a ramrod behind his bar with both hands atop it.

The marshal displayed to Frank what he had heard of him. Even looking straight at the man he only saw a blur as Baca drew. His first shot hit Sage Beaman hard, and although Beaman had been drawing, the six-gun was only half clear of its holster when Beaman was knocked hard against the bar.

Centre Fire growled a curse and braced to fight. His partner did a wise thing, he bumped Centre Fire off balance. Another rangeman, farther up the bar sprang forward and went for his holster. Baca snapped off his second shot. It missed by inches, but rattled the cowboy so that his shot missed and broke the roadside window.

Another rangeman, too young to be seasoned at this sort of thing, fired at the marshal, hit him high in the left leg. Baca struggled for balance as another stockman fired. This time the bullet drew blood across the top of Baca's shoulder and he fell. When he struck the floor his gun skidded away.

Centre Fire said, "You son of a bitch" to his partner, and started toward the wounded man struggling to get to his knees. Centre Fire lowered his weapon, aimed and smiled.

Frank yelled: "Drop it!"

Centre Fire whirled and squeezed the trigger. His bullet splintered the bar behind Frank. He was snapping back the hammer for his second shot when Frank's slug hit him dead centre in the brisket. Centre Fire went sideways and backwards from impact, dead before he finally fell.

For seconds there was no movement until that snarling rangeman whose slug had torn across the marshal's shoulder stepped away from the others with his six-gun hammer being pulled back. Two things happened simultaneously. The townsman standing nearest Frank Zurdo made an unbelievable leap up over the bar where he fell in a heap behind it. The second thing that occurred was when Frank turned slightly sideways as he fired. The rangeman's slug missed Frank and lodged in the southernmost wall of the saloon.

As the snarling man fell Frank quietly said, "Who's next?"

No one was next. Of the five rangemen who had swaggered into the saloon two were still standing. Frank kept his weapon cocked and stone-steady as he said, "You two sons of bitches pick up the marshal and carry him down to the jailhouse. *Now, gawddamnyou!*"

The necessarily loud sound of Henry cocking his scattergun was enough. The rangemen went over to Baca, got him to his feet and led the way out of the saloon with Frank behind them.

There was consternation in the saloon. Only two of the townsmen had been armed; they'd had no idea what they would find when they visited Henry's place for a nightcap. Now, they were all furiously talking at the same time.

At the jailhouse, which was clammy-cold, Frank herded the stockmen with their burden down into the cell-room where they placed Fred Baca on a cot. Frank then disarmed them, locked them in the opposite cell, put up his weapon as he eyed them before he said, "You damned idiots," and went up front to fire-up the little iron wood-stove. The jailhouse hadn't been heated in months.

Frank found the dented speckleware coffeepot, some ground beans and made coffee. While waiting for it to boil he rolled a smoke. His nerves were crawling, he sat at the desk, tipped his hat and glared at the cell-room door. Of all the damned fools he had met Fred Baca was foremost. Anyone, even the village idiot, would have known better than to brace five rangemen at the same time. He wondered if Heatherton had a doctor, and doubted it; few places smaller than a town had one. He was finishing his smoke when someone rapped on the roadway door. Frank drew and cocked his six-gun, held it behind his back and opened the door. The man standing there had the smooth complexion of a baby and a mop of snow white hair. He introduced himself. "I'm Parson Ross of the Baptist church at the upper end of town. I've been called to care for the ill and injured. Would you mind if I looked at the new marshal? I understand he got shot up . . . It sounded like a war. Everyone in town heard it, Mister . . . ?"

"Frank Zurdo, parson. Come along."

Fred Baca, who had never lost consciousness, looked like he had been yanked through a meat grinder; his clothing was blood-soaked, his wounded leg was swelling.

He looked at the rosy-cheeked older

man. Frank said, "He's the town preacher, and whatnot . . . While he's workin' on you I'll get a bottle of whiskey."

Baca nodded weakly and closed his eyes. As Frank walked out of the cell he saw the two cowed rangemen in the opposite cell, he hesitated long enough to say, "Where I come from they'd hang you two bastards from the nearest tree."

One of the stockmen whined, "We didn't know there'd be trouble."

Frank sneered, "You're a liar. You had to know comin' to town with Beaman would make trouble. Mister, I been a rangeman most of my life, I know how bastards like you think. You'd ride into this town behind that big bully and buffalo the town. Naw; not another word, mister."

Frank went up to the office, searched high and low for a bottle, did not find one and wondered what kind of a lawman Heatherton had had before Baca came along. He did not want to go up to the saloon but he did.

The moment he pushed past the spindle doors the room became silent. Frank ignored all the others and spoke to Henry. "A bottle of whiskey, Henry."

As the saloonman handed over the bottle he said, "How is he?"

Frank's answer was short. "I don't know. There's a preacher with him," and walked out of the saloon where, almost before the spindle doors stopped moving, conversation resumed where it had left off when Frank had entered. If he'd stayed he would not have liked what they were discussing. A lynching.

Parson Eli Ross seemed to be one of those quiet people of considerable understanding and efficiency. He had finished with the marshal when Frank arrived and looked in on Baca as the minister was drying his hands. Somewhere he had found a chipped bowl. It was half full of pink water. As he finished with the towel and reached for his coat, he smiled. "He's asleep. I gave him laudanum. There'll be pain but neither of his wounds are very serious. The bone in his leg was not struck but the muscles were torn. It'll be a while before he runs a foot race." As the parson walked out of the cell he also said, "In cases like this, it is infection we have to fear — I'll be back."

Frank held the door and smiled his appreciation. After the minister had departed he returned to the cell room. Fred Baca was breathing deeply. One of the rangemen across the narrow little corridor spoke quietly. "Mister, we'll give you the money if you'll fetch us something to eat."

Frank turned, one of the men was holding forth an upturned hand with silver coins. Frank took the coins, leaned closer and threw them back into the cell. He waited for the protest but it did not come. The reason it didn't was because the rangemen had been holding a lengthy conversation among themselves, the results of which was that whoever the man who carried his gun on the wrong side, had shot twice, had killed both his adversaries dead centre. Maybe he was, as they were, a rangeman as he'd said, but if that was true, they agreed among themselves he was better with a Colt than anyone they'd known. In short, they were afraid of Frank Zurdo.

If he'd known that it would not have bothered him a bit.

He locked the jailhouse and went up to the boarding house where the proprietor met him with a respectful nod and an uneasy smile.

The following morning Frank was still bitter, but he got food for his prisoners at the cafe and took it over to the cell room. He did not say a word as he gestured for the pair of cowboys to go to the back of their cell, after which he opened the door, put the food containers on the floor, backed out and re-locked the door. One man said, "Much obliged, Mister."

Frank's answer was curt. "I don't need your thanks." He glanced over at Baca who was still sleeping, returned to the office, sat down and swore. Everyone was treating him as though he was a lawman, which he'd never been in his life and had never wanted to be.

Damn Baca anyway!

A slightly stooped large, rawboned old man tied up out front and opened the jailhouse door. Frank looked at him. The old man was hard-eyed with a bear trap mouth. He neither nodded or said 'good morning' he went to a chair, hitched his holster around and sat down looking steadily at Frank, whose annoyance was rising by the second. When the large older man did not speak Frank did. "Who the hell are you an' what do you want?"

The old man's voice was not hostile, it was flat and without inflection when he replied. "My name's John Hendrick. Anyone can tell you who I am. What I want is you got two riders locked up an' I want them turned loose. Something else, cowboy. You killed my top hand, a feller we called Centre Fire."

Frank leaned forward on the constable's table, clenched both hands and did not blink. He had known his share of ranchers, quite a few had this man's outlook and disposition. Frank spoke bluntly. "Let me tell you something, old man, your top hand walked over to the downed marshal who had lost his gun and was goin' to shoot him in the head."

The cowman said, "Don't call me old man. I'll have your damned hide."

Frank continued to lean and glare when he went on explaining. "That other son of a bitch — Beaman — started the trouble. If he's your rider you sure didn't show good sense lettin' him come into a town that hates his guts for shootin' down a young feller who was unarmed."

"He was armed," the cowman growled.

Frank shook his head. "Everyone I've talked to said he wasn't armed."

"They're lyin'. These townfolks stick together like glue."

Frank smiled without a shred of warmth when he said, "Old man, I think you're the liar when you say that young feller was armed. The whole damned town can't be wrong. That tame ape of yours killed that feller in front of a saloon full of onlookers. They said he was not armed."

John Hendrick loosened in his chair and his next sentence was softly said. "Mister whatever-your-name is, you just ended this talk when you called me a liar."

Frank stood up. "All right, old man. *Stand up!*"

Hendrick did not leave his chair. He had heard what had happened at the saloon. He instead closed his hands together in his lap where they were in plain sight. He regarded Frank for a long moment before speaking again. "What's your name?"

"Frank Zurdo."

"Mister Zurdo, you don't want me for an enemy."

Frank's ire was fully up. "No, you're right, I don't. I was passin' through when this mess landed in my lap. But old man if you think you scare me, guess again. You want to stand up or do you want to talk?"

John Hendrick did not move. "Turn my riders loose, Mister Zurdo," he said in that soft tone of voice.

"Maybe, when the smoke clears. Until it does they stay in the cell." Frank perched on the edge of the table nearest to the rugged-looking old cowman. "It's not up to me. I'm not the law here; he's yonder in a cell patched up asleep. When he comes around I'll ask him what to do with your riders. Meanwhile, old man, stay out of town and keep your riders out."

Frank went to the door, held it open and jerked his head.

After the rawboned, rugged older

man left, Frank went over to the general store, sought the proprietor and without mentioning his recent visitor, told the storekeeper the town should find someone to take Fred Baca's place until the marshal could resume his duties.

The storekeeper listened to everything Frank said, then took Frank to his cluttered office, sat him down and spoke seriously. "Mister Zurdo, the town wants to lynch those rangemen."

Frank was not as surprised as he was annoyed that the merchant would tell Frank this as though it was Frank's business. He glanced at the small iron stove which was still warm although the fire was dead. When he looked back he spoke bluntly. "This isn't any of my business. I'm just passing through on my way south where it don't snow hip pocket high to a tall In'ian. Mister, you find someone to mind things until the marshal can get back on his feet. I'm leaving in the morning."

Frank left the store annoyed, went

down to the cafe for breakfast and was met by either an approving, or sympathetic, silence by other diners. Only the cafeman was cheerful and talkative. He said, "Mister, what you done last night the town's been wantin' to do for a long time."

Frank was raising his coffee cup when he said, "Lynch 'em?"

Everyone in the room stopped moving. The silence was as taut as a new lariat. The cafeman cleared his throat, got the pot to re-fill Frank's cup, and sounded judgmental when he said, "You don't believe in lynching?"

Frank's reply was short. "If they deserve it I'd lean on a hangrope as quick as you would. But those idiots don't deserve hanging. They're damned fools for lettin' themselves get roped into Beaman's private war with your town." Frank put the cup down. "Gents, leave it be, the marshal'll be all right in time." He looked steadily at the cafeman, who went after Frank's breakfast. Before he had finished the other diners had shuffled out. As he was paying the cafeman he smiled at him. "If folks lynched every damned fool, a man'd have to ride a long time before he met anyone, wouldn't he?"

Out in the clear morning with its hint of frost, Frank went down to the livery barn. The widow-woman met him with a pronouncement. "Your horse's shoes are worn thin. If you figure to ride far you'd better get a new set all around."

Frank went to look at his horse, and swore. She was right. They sure didn't make horseshoes like they used to. The toughest horseshoes were made from the tines of a hay rake, they were light, almost indestructible, and easy to fit.

He was leaning in weak sunshine when the widow-woman came over, looked at Frank's animal and said, "There's a blacksmith across the road behind the ice house."

Frank looked down at her. "I was plannin' on leavin' in the morning."

She looked congenial when she said,

"You still can. I'll take him over there as soon as I'm finished with my chores, an' you can go get him before noon."

Frank smiled. "I'll lead him over, no sense in your havin' to."

Her reply came back quickly. "I have to take two horses over there anyway, one more won't matter."

Frank nodded. "I'm obliged. Thank you."

" . . . Mister Zurdo, what you . . . "

"Frank. Just plain Frank."

She nodded. "I have a terrible memory. Frank . . . What you did at the saloon makes it possible for me to rest easier . . . I was going to do that, someday."

He stared at her, nodded and walked away. She was figuring to kill Sage Beaman? Hell; he'd have made mincemeat out of her.

5

The Best Laid Plans . . .

THE blacksmith was an older man, stringy as rawhide. He chewed and spat frequently but never when women were around. He was tall so he had to look down at Buffy Devon as she spoke, and when she finished, when he normally would have expectorated, he said, "It's close to the truth, ma'm. I really do have work piled up until tomorrow."

If Frank could have heard that discussion he would have told them both off, but he was at the jailhouse feeding his prisoners and visiting Fred Baca, who looked worse but seemed better. He wasn't hungry and Frank refused to fetch him the bottle from the office as he considered the immensely swollen leg and the other wrappings.

He spoke to the marshal as though speaking to himself. "You're not goin' to get up from here for a week, maybe longer.

Baca considered the other man. "That preacher'll look after me."

"Sure; an' who'll look after the damned town? I killed some rangemen, their kind don't take kindly to things like that ... Marshal, that was a downright stupid thing you did — brace five armed men at once.

Baca nodded slightly. "How many are left?"

"Two. Across the way from you."

"Well then someone else had to be just as stupid, didn't they?"

Frank left the marshal, stood briefly in the narrow dingy little corridor gazing at his prisoners. "An old man named Hendrick come by. You fellers work for him?"

The only prisoner with an Adam's-apple bobbed his head. "We hired on to winter feed. I expect he won't like it if we don't get back directly."

Frank nodded about that. "He don't like you bein' in here."

"You goin' to let us out, Mister Zurdo?"

"Yeah, when you smell so bad buzzards'll be circling."

Frank returned to the office, stood a while at the sunk-set little front-wall window looking out. He saw the storekeeper and his clerk loading someone's old ranch rig, and farther north a solitary horse was at the saloon tie-rack.

He went to the desk, sat down and cocked his boots up. There was a distinctly metallic scent to the air. The kind of scent that usually presaged snow. He'd wasted time; first thing in the morning with new shoes all around on his horse, he'd set his back to Heatherton and never look back.

Shortly after noon the storekeeper brought mail over. It was mostly wanted dodgers which Frank ignored, and would not have opened the solitary letter even if Mister Lewis had not stood there pointing to it.

Frank said, "I'll give it to the marshal."

The storekeeper's gaze was fixed on Frank. "He won't be able to do anythin' if it's somethin' the law takes care of. You open it."

Frank arose slowly. "I told you — I'm not the law an' got no wish to be. I'm heading south first thing in the morning."

The storekeeper nodded and departed. He was learning, as were others around Heatherton, that Frank Zurdo could be a very stubborn individual.

Frank was up at the harness works drinking coffee as black as original sin and twice as bitter when a grizzled, stocky man with a close-cropped grey beard walked in, nodded around and dumped some leather traces atop the counter as he said, "The thread's rotten, Wes."

The harness-maker walked over, looked and shook his head. "Them tugs been lyin' in a manure pile. Of course the thread's rotten. What do you want me to do about it?"

"Fix 'em."

"So you can leave 'em lyin' in the manure pile again?"

The stocky man's face was reddening, what could be seen of it. "They wasn't left in no manure pile, you old screwt," he exclaimed.

The old beanpole across the counter raised his eyebrows. "Wasn't they? I sewed them tugs with waxed flax-thread two years ago. Manure-pile acid is about the only thing that'll eat through that kind of thread."

"Well; just fix the damned things, will you?" the stocky man snarled and stamped out of the shop. He turned in the doorway looking testily at Frank. "I know who you are, mister, an' maybe this won't mean anythin' to you, but I just brought a feller named Ed Erskine to town."

The stocky man walked up the duck boards mad enough to chew bullets and spit rust. Frank looked at the harness-maker. "Is he the local stager?"

Wesly Hamilton nodded slowly. "Jess Ames. He used to carry mail for the gov'ment but give that up an' started up a one-man stage and cartage business." The old beanpole hung fire for a moment as though coming slowly to a decision. "Mister; I don't expect you'd know Ed Erskine."

"You'd be right," Frank stated.

"Well; he used to ride in this country, but then he found a way to make better money. He hired out to stock interests up in Wyoming to wipe out sheepmen. He's young an' tough, an' about two-thirds mean."

The harness-maker leaned down on his counter considering Frank from shrewd eyes. "I'm not much of a bettin' man because I hate to lose, but this time no money's involved, so I'll bet a stockman hired him . . . You can guess the rest of it. Three rangemen was killed in town, Mister Zurdo."

Frank glanced up as a horseman

passed at a dead-walk heading south. He recognised him immediately. He was the partner of the rider called Centre Fire whose arm he had deliberately bumped in the saloon.

Frank went to the doorway to watch. The rangeman tied up out front of the general store, was inside about ten minutes before returning to the roadway to stuff groceries, mostly tinned goods, into his saddlebags. As he untied and swung up to ride south Frank saw the tightly-wound bedroll behind his saddle.

He returned to the shop where Wes Hamilton was making coffee. That rider's name had been Jim Flood. Frank accepted the cup of black java. Flood was leaving the country. Maybe he didn't like snow either, and then again maybe he didn't like trouble.

The harness-maker interrupted his thoughts. "We used to have a vigilance committee in town, but the last time we all gathered was maybe four, five years back. I figure, though, I could sort of move around town an' let folks know Erskine's back so's you wouldn't have to face him alone."

Frank put the cup down hard and glared. "I'm leavin' in the damned morning! I was just passin' along on my way south when I rode in here. I don't want to be here when the snow comes. I've had all the damned three-foot snowbanks I want . . . Mister, I only bought in over at the saloon because that son of a bitch was goin' to shoot your marshal in the head when Baca was hurt an' had lost his gun."

The old beanpole was totally unruffled in the face of Frank's ire. "It wasn't just Centre Fire was it? . . . Well, you ride on; folks'll understand. No one wants to be around when Ed Erskine is in town. A man's got to think of his own hide, for a fact."

One thing Heatherton should have suspected by now was that once Frank Zurdo got fired up, it took just about as long for him to get calmed down, but in fact he didn't fire up easily, but when he did, as he did now listening to the harness-maker, he showed it in his eyes and words. He gazed steadily and stonily at the older man as he spoke.

"Ed Erskine my butt, you old goat. I'm leavin' in the morning because I figured to before that stager walked in."

"Sure," old Hamilton agreed. "Don't get your feathers ruffled. Like I said, folks'll understand." The older man straightened up off his counter. "Hell, I just remembered somethin'. Ed was after Buffy Devon like a ruttin' buck before he left town to go north. Now that she's a widder-woman an' all . . . with a good business," he leaned back down atop the counter, as sad-eyed as a sick pup. "I expect some of us old fellers can look out for her. Most of us have lived long enough anyway. I've heard Ed Erskine's greased lightin' with a belt-gun."

Frank went down to the cafe in a foul mood and it showed. Diners nodded but said nothing. Even the cafeman said little as he got the pails of food for Baca and the prisoners across the road.

What the marshal asked for was water; a bucketful of it. Frank got the full bucket and a dipper before placing the marshal's food near the cot. He went over across the little corridor, snarled his prisoners to the back of their cell, went in, put the little pails on the floor, straightened up and glared. "They want to lynch you . . . It's all right with me. I'll ride out an' leave the door unlocked."

The rider with the big Adam's-apple squawked, "Fer chris' sake, Mister Zurdo, that ain't human."

"Neither is gangin' up five to one. Shut up, I'm not in the mood. There's your grub; make it last. I may not be back until tomorrow."

He slammed the door, locked it, threw a final sulfurous glare at the stiff-standing rangemen, went up to the office, barred the cell-room from his side, rummaged for that bottle he'd acquired at the saloon and sat down at the desk.

Son of a bitch!

Regardless that he'd told everyone around town who would listen that he'd just been passing through and figured to be on his way, he knew what folks would think, and what they would say the moment he turned his back on Heatherton and kept on riding.

He swallowed twice from the bottle, stoppered it, shoved it into a drawer and went to work making a smoke. *Buffy!* Some two-bit gunman after her, and her without a husband . . . Some old men like that stringbean at the harness works . . . They'd be about as helpful to her as teats on a man.

Later, having simmered down a little but not a lot, he went over for supper at the cafe. The counter was crowded but he found a seat between the preacher and the storekeeper. The preacher smiled benignly while holding his coffee cup aloft. "He's doin' very well. No sign of infection yet. I wash him real good with carbolic acid twice a day."

Frank gave his order and ignored the preacher.

The storekeeper smiled as he said, "Folks put a lot of store by you, Mister Zurdo."

This time there was a reply. "Maybe they won't tomorrow. I'm leavin' as soon as I can rig out my horse in the morning."

The cafeman, leaning to place Frank's platter in front of him, stopped moving. Other customers up and down the counter also seemed to have turned to stone. Frank took the platter, put it in place, reached for his eating utensils and went to work. Someone up the counter softly said, "Ed Erskine's in town."

Frank leaned, searching for that speaker but whoever he was, the others were resuming eating; there was no way to tell. Maybe it hadn't been an innuendo but to Frank it sounded like one.

Later, with shadows forming, he went up to the saloon. There were no more than three or four men at the bar. When Frank walked in silence settled like a pall, only Henry Bolton nodded, said something about having the town carpenter in today to patch things up, and brought Frank's beer, which Frank glowered at as he said, "Whiskey!"

Henry hurried for a bottle and glass. When he set them up he said, "How's the marshal?"

Frank refrained from answering until he'd downed his jolt and had pushed both bottle and glass away. "The minister says he's doing well, but he looks like hell to me . . . What'd you do with the bodies, Henry?"

"Mister Hendrick sent in a wagon for them. They went around to the back alley." Henry made a tentative smile. "I don't think they wanted you to see rangemen in town. The two fellers with the rig never said ten words; we loaded 'em an' they turned around and never looked back. You're gettin' respect, Frank."

An emboldened townsman up the bar spoke loudly. "From what I've heard that new constable ain't goin' to be fit to do his job for a long time, Mister Zurdo. A couple of us was discussin' maybe you'd sort of fill in until — "

Frank's anger returned in a rush. "For the last gawdamned time I'm goin' to tell you I was just passin' through and I'm leavin' first thing in the morning."

The silence returned, deeper than ever. Even Henry said no more. Frank finished his business at the saloon and went up to the boarding house to bed down. He wanted to get an early start; wanted to put Heatherton behind him once and for all, and if he ever had to pass through this area again he was going to go so far out and around the town he couldn't even see the damned rooftops!

The proprietor, another scrawny

old turkey-necked individual like the harness-maker, met Frank in the hall. He neither greeted Frank nor prefaced what he had to say with the ordinary scraps of polite conversation.

"Mister Zurdo, I ain't armed. I haven't carried a gun in fifteen years . . . I don't like to say this an' I hope you'll understand, but years back I've had roomers who was in trouble an' a couple of times the house got shot up . . . You understand?"

"You want me out?" Frank asked, and the older man nodded. He watched Frank the way a hypnotised bird watches a snake.

Frank smiled coldly. "First thing in the morning," he said and marched past to his room, entered, slammed the door and went to stand by the room's only window, which faced south. He could see all the way to the lower end of town where a pair of carriage lamps burned brightly at the livery barn.

There should be a way for a man to know which towns to stay out of, but of course that wasn't possible. He sat on the edge of the bed, kicked out of his boots, draped his gun and shell-belt over the back of the only chair, got ready to bed down, blew down the lamp mantle, climbed in with both eyes wide open.

He should have left the same day he entered Heatherton. He'd only wanted to sleep up off the ground and eat a decent cooked meal or two.

He couldn't blame the town; he had done what he had thought was right and needed doing. But if he'd had even an inkling ... but he hadn't had and now it was too late to change anything.

Heatherton could catch on fire tomorrow and providing the fire didn't start until he was ready to ride, it could burn to the ground and he wouldn't look back.

He punched the ancient pillow, rolled up onto his side — and remembered what the harness-maker had said about Buffy Devon and the troublesome gent named Erskine. He did not dwell upon what the old beanpole had hinted at: Erskine being hired by stockmen to settle with Frank. He'd be gone before Erskine rolled out of his blankets in the morning. But the blue-eyed girl — woman-widow at the lower end of town — *that* bothered him.

Normally Frank, like most men whose lives were spent out of doors, slept like a log. This particular night he didn't. But sometime during the dark hours he must have because a rooster crowing not far from his window made both eyes open.

Day was breaking. Frank looked out the window, saw the brightening sky and swore as he got dressed and hiked out back to the wash-house. It had been his intention to be on his way by now. The sun was coming; he wouldn't be able to leave Heatherton until full daylight now, which annoyed him.

He bypassed the cafe with its fogged-over roadway window, got down to the livery barn as the proprietor was dragging a chair over to blow out the carriage lamps. He waited until she had finished and turned to face him. She smiled as though she hadn't a care in the world, led the way down the gloomy runway to the harness room, sat down and looked Frank straight in the eyes when she told her lie. Someday Frank might learn that female-women were much better liars than men.

"The blacksmith was awful busy yesterday. But I went back after supper last night." She shook her head sympathetically. "He had the shoes pulled but said he couldn't do the re-shoeing until this morning."

6

With Time Running Out

FRANK didn't say it until he was out front where she couldn't hear him: "Son of a bitch!"

He went over to the cafe with its steamy window. It was too early for most cafe diners but there were several puffy-eyed, dour looking men at the counter who barely looked up when Frank entered.

The cafeman gazed pensively as he said, "Folks figured you'd be gone by now, Mister Zurdo."

"Fetch me coffee first then meat, spuds, an' pie if you got any . . . So did I."

The other diners were hunched like crows on a fence. Only one man spoke. "The damned sun's comin'," he said, as though the sun was his personal enemy.

Another diner grunted. That was the extent of conversation until Frank was half through his breakfast when the stocky, bearded, short-tempered stager walked in, sat down next to Frank, ordered in a gruff voice and welcomed his black java with both hands. After half draining the cup he spoke quietly to Frank without looking at him. "Ed was at the hotel askin' about you."

Frank swallowed before saying, "Ed who?"

The testy man turned. "Ed Erskine! If you're fixin' to leave I wouldn't waste a lot of time."

Frank ate, drank coffee, ate until he had to swab meat juice with a scrap of bread to get it all, then waited for the cafeman to re-fill his cup and move along before he said, "One time when I was a button I read a story about some king or other losin' a battle because he couldn't get a horse."

The burly man turned slowly. He did not say a word, he just stared.

"The town blacksmith pulled my

horse's shoes last night an' can't get around to re-shoein' him for awhile."

The man with the close-cropped beard faced forward and went to work on his breakfast. He had nothing to say to someone being hunted by a gunman and who talked about fairy-book stories.

More diners drifted in. Daylight was breaking and while not many folks noticed it, the temperature was rising. This was going to be one of those rare autumn days of golden leaves, unseasonal warmth, and the kind of visibility that let folks see all the way to tomorrow.

Frank went out front, rolled and lighted a quirley, gazed the length of the roadway, crossed over and hiked down to the livery barn.

Buffy Devon was rosy-cheeked and breathing hard, forking feed was not especially hard work for a man, but it was for a female-woman. Without speaking Frank found a second three-tined fork and lent a hand. She smiled but said nothing until they were finished and he was leaning on the fork as he said he thought he'd go over and see how the blacksmith was coming along.

She nodded and also leaned on the fork-handle watching him leave.

The sinewy blacksmith was sitting on a propped-back chair enjoying his first cud of Mule Shoe of the day. He did not see Frank until the other man was standing directly in front of him.

He regarded Frank solemnly for a moment then simultaneously arose from the chair and expectorated before saying, "You'd be Mister Zurdo?"

Frank nodded. The cross-ties were hanging, there was no horse inside the shed, the forge wasn't fired up and the smith did not have his apron on.

"Well, sir, I just et an' it's my policy to let breakfast settle. You'll understand."

Frank eyed the older man. "Miz Devon brought my horse over last evening."

"Yes. Yes she did, an' I pulled his shoes, but it was gettin' late'n the light ain't too good in here of an evening. I figure to finish trimmin' and shoein' him this morning." The blacksmith politely turned aside to spray amber in the direction of the forge. He continued speaking as he faced Frank. "I don't expect you'd know Mister Ames, he owns the local stage and dray company." The blacksmith pointed. "He brought in them two wheels last evenin', an' he's got to have 'em today. The spokes is loose, some are cracked. Mister Ames's only got one stage . . . You'll understand, Mister Zurdo."

Frank continued to look at the blacksmith as he said, "You're going to fix the wheels before you shoe my horse?"

"Well now, Mister Ames's got to keep pretty much to his stagin' schedule. Folks depend on that, an' I don't expect you got to have your horse shod right away . . . I sort of promised

Mister Ames. You'll understand. He's got the only stage runnin' in an' out of town."

Frank said, "How long before you shoe my horse?"

"Oh, considerin' all things, Mister Zurdo, an' assumin' them wheels don't make me no problems, I should be through with them by — maybe noon. Maybe a tad later. That's when I'll do the horse for you ... You'll understand; I only got two hands. But take my word for it, Mister Zurdo, as soon as I can get to it, I'll shoe him."

Frank returned to the roadway. The sun was climbing, the sky was pure blue, visibility was so good he could distinguish trees along the rim of the distant northerly mountains.

"Son of a bitch!"

Across the road he saw Buffy Devon raking out front. She smiled and called. "He's pretty busy, Mister Zurdo."

Frank rolled and lighted a smoke, leaned against an upright gazing over at her. Busy blacksmiths don't sit on their backsides and make up stories about letting their breakfasts settle. Buffy finished raking and disappeared down the runway. And livery-barn ladies don't go over to the smithy with no reason after supper to ask if someone's horse would be shod. Maybe for a friend she might; not for a stranger.

And — they didn't call over that a blacksmith was busy when he was sitting relaxed.

Frank crossed the road and entered the runway. Buffy greeted him with a broad smile. "Isn't it a beautiful day? I love In'ian summers like this, don't you?"

He sat on a wall-bench gazing at her gently shaking his head as he spoke. "I've never been in a town like this before."

Her eyes twinkled at him. "It's a nice place . . . Most of the time." Her smile faded, her eyes dropped from his face.

He did not have the heart to say what he had figured out, which was simply that the old-time king who had lost his behind because of a horse, and Frank Zurdo had something in common. He wondered if the old-time king had been weaseled-around the way this girl-woman had done, in collusion with that damned blacksmith.

He walked out front into warming sunlight. Three riders were approaching town from the south. He ignored them to stroll up to the jailhouse.

Fred Baca's leg was about the size of a small beer keg. The parson had split his trousers. He looked like hell but he smiled when Frank entered the cell. "As long as I lie real still nothin' hurts."

Frank pulled up a three-legged stool as he asked if the marshal was hungry. Baca was and barely inclined his head as he said, "Yes. So are the pigs across the hall. They been callin' you some uncomplimentary names."

Frank arose. "I'll fetch you some

grub," he said, and walked across the little corridor to look in at the prisoners, who looked dirty, unshaven, and unhappy. He asked a question. "Which one of you cussed me out to the marshal?"

The man with the prominent Adam's-apple scowled. "We didn't cuss you out. We said a feller could starve to death in here, an' our commode pot needs emptyin'. That's all."

Baca spoke in a surprisingly strong voice. "You lyin' bastard!"

The cowboy seemed to have lost the ability to respond. He looked at his companion, would not face Frank again. Frank considered them; if ever two human beings looked worn down and haggard those men did. Even at their best they hadn't looked like the kind of individuals Frank would have cared to know.

Up front someone opened the roadway door and slammed it after himself. Frank walked up out of the cell room and stopped in his tracks with the door at his back still open.

His visitor was that old cowman named Hendrick and two unsmiling, rugged-looking riders. Hendrick wasted no words. "Turn 'em loose."

Frank turned, closed and barred the door at his back, crossed to the desk and set his back to it as he replied. "It's not up to me — old man — it's up to the marshal."

Hendrick's craggy face coloured. No one as old as he was liked being reminded of it, particularly by what he thought of as some grub line rider. He stood legs spread, both arms hanging loose. The rangemen behind him scarcely blinked in their steady regard of the man who wore his gun on the wrong side. The older man stood like stone, seemingly weighing something in his mind. For a fact no man lived as long as John Hendrick had lived by being a fool; if a fight started in the jailhouse office, a room less than fifteen feet square, the odds were considerable that he would die here. It wasn't a matter of courage, it was a matter of common sense.

Frank spoke again. "Did you send a man named Ed Erskine to look me up, Mister Hendrick?"

The old man's eyes flickered away then back. Frank nodded his head. "You did. Old man, why didn't you look me up yourself? Fingers too stiff, muscles too puny, backbone too yeller?"

One of the rangemen snarled at Frank. "You pushed your luck too far, grub-liner."

That was the problem in a situation like this; there was usually someone too hot-headed to use his brain if he had one. This was how killings happened. Hendrick growled at his rider without looking away from Frank. "I told you — I'd do the talkin'."

The cowboy was quiet but his stare at Frank was deadly. Hendrick said it again. "Turn 'em loose."

Whatever Frank might have said was never spoken. Someone violently kicked the roadway door open. The tense men inside could not help starting in surprise. A reedy voice gave them an order. "Don't move!"

There were three of them, every man-jack with a shotgun. At that range shotguns tore bodies to pieces. One of them was the beanpole from the harness works. Another one was the testy stager with the close-cropped beard. The third one was the sinewy blacksmith whose worn-smooth muleskin apron hung past his knees. He spat without turning his head.

The harnessman spoke again in his reedy voice. "Mister Zurdo, disarm 'em."

Frank went over to lift their handguns. He gave the belligerent cowboy a sharp poke in back over the kidneys as he told him to sit on a wall bench. The other two riders joined him over there. John Hendrick was staring at the men with scatterguns on the plankwalk outside when Frank reached, got a fistful of cloth, swung the old man violently against a wall, left him and crossed back to the desk.

The reedy voice said, "You want 'em, Mister Zurdo? If you don't the town's ready to hang them other two, an' since we can't get into no more trouble for hangin' five men than two, we'll take 'em."

Frank let the rangemen worry a moment or two before saying he would lock them up along with their friends. The bearded stager growled about that. "What good'll that do? Our way, it'll get settled once an' for all."

Frank did not dispute this, he simply said, "I'm obliged, gents," and closed the door in their faces.

He rolled and lighted a smoke. The stockmen watched his every move. He sat down at the desk gazing at them when he addressed John Hendrick. "I don't expect a measly old son of a bitch like you would realise it, but I just saved your damned bacon . . . You picked a poor time to ride into town. They've been talkin' about lynching the other two for a couple of days. I don't know 'em real well, but as far as I'm concerned they can hang you anytime."

The rangeman who had heretofore been silent, said, "You got any idea what would happen? Every cowman for a hunnert miles would come to Heatherton with their riders. There wouldn't be much left."

Frank shook his head at the speaker. "I've ridden for a lot of cow outfits. Not one in fifty that I know of would buy into the mess you gents are cookin' up."

Hendrick said, "The army'd come."

Frank nodded about that and spoke quietly. "Most likely, but you fellers wouldn't be around to see 'em ride in." Frank arose and gestured in the direction of the cell room. They stood back until he had opened it then trooped one behind the other down where three stone-still and silent looked on as Frank locked the three newcomers into the same cell, which was opposite

Baca's cell and adjoined the cell of their friends.

He did not say a word but as he passed the marshal's cell he and Fred Baca exchanged a wink.

Frank draped the six-guns taken from Hendrick and his riders from nails in the back wall. He didn't speculate on how the shotgun-men had come to be out front but it would not have been hard to figure; the town undoubtedly saw those three rangemen enter from the south and tie up out front of the jailhouse. The rest of it would be elementary enough.

He left the jailhouse and for the first time locked the door from the outside. There were people on both sides of the road; it was that kind of a day. Autumn did not always present people with golden displays of last final vestiges of summer, but when it did, what folks called 'Indian summer', could stay for several days, occasionally for weeks but that was nothing to bet on.

Frank crossed to the general store

where the moon-faced proprietor looked mildly startled. The place was alive with customers. He lingered long enough to buy a sack of Bull Durham then strolled northward in the direction of the saloon.

From across the road the saddlemaker appeared out front wagging his head. Frank nodded, smiled and entered the saloon where he got an almost identical look, but without the head-wag from Henry Bolton.

There were several old men sitting by a front window soaking up warmth. Occasionally one would rouse himself to speak and the others would rouse themselves to listen, then to go back to dozing.

There were even some blue-tailed flies circulating in the room. Sooner or later they would bump a window.

Henry had red suspenders holding up his britches. He looked self-conscious when he caught Frank looking at them and said, "My wife's idea. She says it annoys her to see me hitchin' up my pants so often, so she bought these things. She says I'm gettin' too big in the gut. Well, I told her in my business about all the exercise a man gets is fillin' glasses an' fetchin' bottles."

Frank nodded for beer as he continued to admire the red suspenders. He told the saloonman they looked good on him. Henry eyed Frank askance; he'd been serving rangemen for too many years not to understand dead-pan teasing when he encountered it. Henry changed the subject. "I missed the fun out front of the jailhouse. What did you do with 'em?"

"Locked 'em up," Frank replied as he raised the beer glass.

Henry waited until the glass was lowered to say, "It's pretty much cow country, Frank. The news'll get around an' you know how stockmen react to somethin' like this."

"Henry, has Erskine been in today? I heard he was at the hotel lookin' for me."

"He was in after breakfast. I haven't

seen him since. You want some advice, Frank?"

"No, but I'll have another beer."

After his second beer was brought Frank blew out a big sigh. "By rights I should be five miles south by now . . . Henry, her an' that blacksmith let me walk right into a trap. He didn't shoe my horse this morning an' I'll lay you a year's pay she put him up to it."

Bolton made a wide sweep of his bartop with a rag he kept tucked into his waist. "Women are sly critters for a fact. I expect they got to be since they can't shoot straight nor knock a man down." Henry smiled. "Wait until you marry one, you'll see what I mean."

"Might be a long wait," Frank replied, and counted out silver coins which he placed beside the empty glass. As he was turning he said, "What's Erskine look like? I never liked bein' surprised."

"He's about your size and heft, packs an ivory-stocked Colt, got a hairline that's farther back now than when I first met him. He dresses better'n most cowmen who can afford it better'n I think he can."

"When he was in did he ask about me?"

"No. Not a question. In fact he hardly talked at all. I'll tell you one thing; he ain't the same man he was ten years back."

"None of us are, Henry. If we was you wouldn't be wearin' them red suspenders."

Outside the day was almost warm enough to pass for a summer day, except for the obvious signs of late autumn, which were most noticeable on the trees around town. Their colour was predominantly gold, with a few russet, bright yellow and scarlet leaves.

Frank crossed to the harness works and leaned in the doorway watching people in greater numbers than he had seen before in Heatherton. Some did not even wear coats or sweaters.

From deeper in the shop a voice said,

"Saved your bacon, we did. Why'n hell did you let all three of 'em inside?"

Frank turned. "I didn't know they were in town."

"What'd you do with 'em?"

"Locked 'em up."

The harness-maker chuckled. "Mister Kendrick won't like that even a little bit. He's a big In'ian in these parts."

"What's Ed Erskine look like?" Frank asked, and got an almost identical description as the one he had gotten over at the saloon, before the harnessman said something else.

"He'll be lookin' for you down at the livery barn. By now he knows you keep a horse down there — an' he'll have another reason for goin' down there ... Buffy Devon ... Frank be gawda'mighty careful. Anyone who hired out during the sheep war up in Wyoming didn't make his money facin' 'em down. That kind kills any way they can, from ambush, from behind skirts. You be careful, us old fellers can't keep on coverin' your butt."

Frank smiled at the old beanpole. "I'm real obliged for what you gents did at the jailhouse, but don't try it again . . . You might get yourself shot."

Old Hamilton leaned on his cutting table looking at Frank as he replied. "You leave me thinkin' you got more sand in your craw than brains in your head . . . All right; good luck but be gawdawful careful."

7

One Mistake

FRANK had not come down in the last rain, nor had his mammy, whoever and wherever she was, spawned a fool.

Frank went around to the back alley and walked toward the lower end of town. There was some little nubbin in a man's mind that warned when danger was close. In this case Frank did not have to speculate; that old bastard in the jailhouse had sure as hell as not, hired a troublesome back-shooter to kill him.

If Erskine was at the livery barn Frank's idea was not to walk onto him in that gloomy runway when Erskine's eyes would be adjusted to gloom and Frank's wouldn't be.

A sorrel dog who looked half as big

as a small pony came out of a hole in a dilapidated fence like he'd been shot out of a cannon. Frank saw him and stopped stone still. The dog did not stop. He was snarling. An old man came through the same old fence with a walking staff. He swore at the dog and limped forward with his stick raised. He might as well have been on the moon. The dog had Frank's leg in sight.

The old man raised his voice. "Don't move, mister. Stand real still. He'll only attack if someone moves."

Frank obeyed. He'd been gauging distance to kick the big dog in the ribs, but he obeyed the old man, assuming he owned the damned dog and knew what he was talking about, but it took courage; the dog stopped about eight inches from Frank, snarled, hair-stiff along his back, eyes fixed and fiery. He slobbered a little, backed up a short distance and hunkered. He was getting poised to leap and attack.

Frank moved, just his left hand. It

was within inches of his holster when the old man hit the dog with the gnarled knob on the upper end of his walking stick. The dog collapsed as though he'd been shot.

The old man stopped beside the unconscious dog looking at Frank. "I apologise. I usually keep him in the shack with me or on a chain. Now'n then we go for a walk. Mister, you did just right, and I admire you for that; he ain't an animal folks usually don't move around."

Frank looked at the dog. "You hit him pretty hard."

The old man looked down and wagged his head. "No harder'n other times. Old Matt's got a skull half inch thick. I'm real sorry he scairt you."

Frank raised his eyes. The dog's owner was big and rawboned; at one time, maybe forty years back he'd been an individual a man wouldn't care to cross. Now, he was old, slightly bent, lined and raggedly dressed, but his eyes were as clear as glass, faded, maybe a tad watery, but piercing.

Frank loosened, looking at the dog, who was breathing in even, deep sweeps. He shook his head. "Someone'll shoot him, mister."

"I live in the shack beyond that broke-down fence. Only lately has he been able to shove through. I'll get the fence fixed. I sure apologise for him, mister."

Frank left them in the alley and resumed his way southward. The big old man leaned, swore at his dog and got ready to wait. It usually only required about ten minutes for the dog to recover, and for a fact when he was back through the fence on his chain he would sleep most of the day. The old man always dosed him with whiskey after knocking him senseless; whether it ameliorated the headache or not it surely made the dog sleep.

Over at the smithy someone was warping steel over an anvil, a pleasant sound, in the corral where Frank's horse had been kept there was a span of big young Missouri mules; they were worth a small fortune. They watched Frank coming down the alley, moved to the alley-side of the corral and, mule-like, stood side by side, big ears pointing, gravely watching the two-legged creature until Frank moved closer to their side of the alley, then they sidled away but still watched him.

Frank heard voices as he was sidling along the alley-side wall of the barn in the direction of the doorless wide runway which ran the full length of the barn.

The voices stopped as he was near the north side of the opening. When they started again Frank could distinguish every word. A man said, "I'd have took care of the son of a bitch for you, Buffy. If I'd come back sooner . . . I knew Beaman. I'd have socked him away for you."

The female voice spoke without much inflection. "I'd as leave not talk about it, Ed."

"Why not? It was done."

"Because I don't like Clary bein' mentioned by you, that's why."

For seconds there was no more talk, then the man spoke again. "Buffy, I got money. I figure to go east, settle in some nice town . . . We was friends once, remember?"

This time she did not respond.

The man's voice acquired an edge. "You can't go on runnin' a livery barn. It ain't ladylike. Folks'll talk."

This time she spoke sharply. "This business was what me'n Clary dreamed about; ownin' a way to make a livin'. I don't care what folks say, an' I don't think they say anythin' anyway. Heatherton's a decent town."

"All right, we'll stay here. I'll get them old corrals rebuilt, we can expand across the alley, get some rigs to hire out, store winter feed, maybe get into the haulin' business."

She did not speak. Frank inched to the edge of the alley opening. His shoulder rattled an old warped board. In the silence that sound carried. He stepped forward facing up the runway. Buffy and the man with the ivory-stocked gun stared at him. She recovered swiftly and called to Frank. "Mister Jones I'll get your horse."

Frank nodded as he walked steadily up the runway. Ed Erskine was faintly frowning. When less than fifty feet separated them Erskine said, "Mister, we was havin' a personal little talk. She can get your horse when we're through."

Frank stopped walking. "My name's Frank Zurdo, not Jones."

He watched surprise come over Erskine's face. During the seconds required for the gunman to realise Buffy Devon had deliberately fooled him, Frank spoke again.

"I got the man who hired you an' a couple of his riders in the jailhouse."

Buffy Devon seemed to have turned to stone. She had one hand across her mouth, her eyes were perfectly round. She was scarcely breathing.

Frank's next words were curt. "Buffy, get over against the wall. *Move!*"

She obeyed but only when Frank's last word sounded like a whiplash.

Ed Erskine had the tie-down thong holding his sidearm in its holster. Frank nodded, "Pull the tie-down loose, Mister Erskine."

The gunman made a scarcely discernible wag of his head. "No."

Frank said, "*Do it!* After that it's up to you. I'll wait."

Ed Erskine's tongue made a swift slide over his lips. He made no move toward his tie-down thong, Frank waited; he had seen this happen before. Fired-up men fought, often regardless of the odds, the way Fred Baca had done at the saloon, but men caught by surprise usually hung-fire. For a fact when they talked they did not fight.

Frank watched the gunman's expression change. Erskine said, "I got no quarrel with you, Zurdo. Hendrick has, I don't."

Frank let his breath out slowly. "Reach around with your left hand, pull the thong loose and drop the gun — or use it."

Erskine moved very slowly as he obeyed. When he dropped the ivory-stocked six-gun he said, "I told him it wasn't worth no hunnert dollars to settle with you over Sage Beaman."

"Is that a fact? Then why was you stalkin' around town lookin' for me?" When Erskine did not reply Frank said, "Walk up front, I'll be behind you. Turn left an' go up as far as the jailhouse."

As the gunman turned to obey Frank risked a quick glance at Buffy. She was as white as a sheet.

Outside the beautiful warm day had a faint scent of dead flowers and cured grass. Over in front of the general store several women with shopping bags on their arms saw Frank herding Ed Erskine. They turned and watched. Farther along that old beanpole who owned the leather works was out front on his bench soaking up sunshine. His head came up and around like a turtle's. He stood up and used wide strides in the direction of the saloon.

At the jailhouse Frank growled for Erskine to move north as Frank opened the door. Bush-whackers were experienced in waiting for their chance. As Frank leaned to unlock the door someone over in front of the general store loudly squawked. It was too late.

The shot was surprisingly loud from such a small belly-gun, except that it was a .44 calibre with one barrel above and one below.

Frank had an instantaneous sensation of something red hot inside his body. He fell sideways, sprawled over a bench and felt dazed and sick without losing consciousness. His vision was blurred. Erskine straddled him, jerked loose Frank's six-gun, fired a shot in the direction of the general store which hit no one but which shattered the big glass window in the front wall, and as people ran for cover, one woman toppled over in a dead faint and another woman, thinking the fainted woman had been shot, let go with a wailing scream that reached to the north end of town.

Buffy heard the shot from mid-way down her runway. She started to run toward the roadway barn opening. She almost made it when a running man waving a six-gun, barreled into her. As she went down she saw the contorted face of Ed Erskine as he sprang past.

She rolled over. Erskine was yanking a horse from a stall. He tied the shank and ran into the harness room for a bridle. It was too large, he swore as he fumbled at the adjusting buckles. The horse, a placid, willing, honest animal, was infected by Erskine's frenzy and set back, something it had never done before. Erskine kicked its rump to bring it up so he could free the tethering shank. The horse came forward with rolling eyes and distended nostrils.

Somewhere up the roadway men were shouting. Buffy got up on all fours, the collision had not caused damage but it had momentarily disoriented her.

She watched Erskine yank the horse around to spring on it bareback. He saw her staring and snarled. "That dumb son of a bitch." He sprang astride, yanked the horse around and fled out the rear of the barn.

She got upright, beat dust off and went out front. There was a crowd in front of the jailhouse. She wanted to go up there but her legs would not move. She knew what had happened without being told. Erskine had somehow shot Frank Zurdo.

She sought a place to sit and watched the activity, was still sitting there when the crowd moved inside the jailhouse. She could not see who they were carrying but she did not have to.

Someone came over and sat beside her. Normally she could have guessed who it was by the scent of chewing tobacco. Right at this moment she was only scarcely aware someone was sitting there.

The blacksmith said, "He had a

big-bore derringer. I expect it's easy to say now Mister Zurdo should have searched him."

They sat in silence until the blacksmith arose and hiked in the direction of his shoeing shed. One thing was sure fact: He wouldn't have to worry about shoeing Mister Zurdo's horse for a while. Maybe never.

Buffy went to her harness room and sat there until late afternoon feeling numb. It only gradually came to her that she was responsible. If she hadn't schemed to keep Frank in town it would not have happened . . . First her husband, then Frank. Heatherton was a murderer's town.

When the beautiful golden day was dying Jess Ames tooled his old stage into town from the south and noticed something he'd never seen before. With shadows lengthening the pair of carriage lamps on each side of the livery barn doorway had not been lighted. In Jess Ames' experience this had not happened since the Devons had owned the livery barn. The stocky stager had a premonition; he stopped in the middle of the road, climbed down and went down the darkening runway calling Buffy's name.

She was slumped over the rickety old harness-room table sobbing when Jess looked in. Without a word he lighted the lamp, hung it from its ceiling wire, gazed at the girl-woman and cleared his throat. He was not a married man. In fact he never much bothered about female-women, and right now he was uncomfortable. Buffy raised a tear-stained face. The gruff stager did something by instinct he would never have done otherwise. He took one of the limp small hands and held it. "What happened?" he asked.

"Ed Erskine shot Frank Zurdo an' it's my fault."

Someone out front was bellowing like a bay steer because the stage was blocking the road. Ames went out there, snarled at the pair of riders who were indignant, climbed aloft and drove up to his yard.

Later, he heard what had happened. For a fact a deaf and dumb person would have heard the story by late sundown.

The harness-maker was over at Bolton's saloon where anger prevailed. Four townsmen had gone after Erskine but with dusk settling and a moonless night to follow, the patrons of Henry's place were not hopeful.

After an hour of cursing and making threats someone put forth the notion which they all would have come around to sooner or later.

"Hang 'em," a townsman said. "We should have done it yestiddy. Hang the whole damned lot of them. That old billy goat named Hendrick first."

There was not a single dissenting voice. "Killed young Devon who wasn't armed, an' now back-shot the cowboy who saved the marshal's hide too . . . From behind with a damned hide-out pistol . . . Start out with them bastards at the jailhouse. Later, when they bring Erskine back, him too."

The beanpole from across the road dryly said, "*If* they bring Erskine back. There's no moon tonight an' he got a fair head start."

No one was willing to accept the possibility that Erskine would not be brought back. Henry was sweating like a stud horse keeping up with the demands of his customers. He agreed with everything they said. He paused in front of the stager to ask if anyone knew how bad off Frank was. The burly bearded man's reply was listened to in abrupt silence.

"He's alive. The parson says he got hit pretty hard at close range ... If he recovers it'll not be for a while." The stager lowered his voice. "*If* he recovers. I saw him ... he looked like a stuck hawg. There was even blood in his boots when I pulled 'em off ... Buffy's takin' it real hard."

No one asked why that was but the old beanpole from the harness works rolled his eyes.

The day of autumn gold ended, warmth was gradually replaced by night-cold. Lights burned throughout town but most noticeable down at the jailhouse where Parson Ross had the front door barred to keep folks out, some of whom drifted down from the saloon breathing flammable breath and making grisly predictions.

Fred Baca, propped on one arm, watched in silence as the preacher worked over Frank Zurdo, who had been dosed with enough laudanum to keep him in deep slumber until morning which provided the parson with ample time to snip away torn flesh, dig out the slug, staunch the bleeding and rest between chores. He sat on a three-legged little stool looking across at the marshal. Baca said, "Will he make it?"

The parson wanly smiled. "If you believe in miracles . . . I do. I've seen miracles happen."

Baca was checked up short for a response. He knew nothing of miracles.

He was a practical individual. The parson spoke again. "He must have been bending when he was shot. I'd say except for that he would have been killed on the spot . . . The bullet went across his back like a knife, then went deeper. It was pushing against the skin where I dug it out. There was powder-burn even through his clothing in his back. That's got to be dug out too, but not until he's able to stand it."

"But he'll live?" Baca asked.

The parson shrugged narrow shoulders. "He is in the hands of God, Mister Baca."

Baca twisted as much as he could to look across the dingy little corridor. "You better pray he don't die. If he does I'm goin' to open you bastards up like a gutted chicken."

The man with the prominent Adam's-apple squeaked his reply. "It wasn't us, for chris' sake. We been locked in here for days. It was — them," the cowboy pointed toward the cell holding John Hendrick and his two rangemen.

Baca ignored that, but he shifted his attention to Hendrick and his riders in the adjoining cell. They looked back without sound or expression. "Right now I'd give good money for the use of a shotgun for a few minutes," Baca exclaimed.

Parson Ross stood up to wash both hands in the pink water of a small basin. He intended to sit with Frank until morning if need be. It worried him that Frank had lost so much blood. Up to a point a man could survive blood loss, beyond that point he couldn't, and Frank had looked like a butchered beef when the parson had been summoned to the jailhouse.

It was, as he had said, in the hands of God.

8

A Bad Night

IT was late, past ten o'clock. Most of Heatherton had bedded down hours before, but there was still an occasional light among the residences while along Front Street, as it was called, even the saloon was dark.

Parson Ross was asleep in a chair he had brought from the office. He heard nothing but Fred Baca did. He listened to be sure, then growled the preacher awake. "Someone's out front," he said. "Be careful, it could be lynchers. There's a shotgun in the rack on the wall."

The minister walked up to the office, waited until he heard the knocking again, then ignored Baca's advice and opened the door. If it had been lynchers . . . but it was Buffy Devon wrapped in an old sheep-pelt coat two sizes too big.

He stepped aside for her to enter and a gust of cold air made the lamp hanging from the ceiling waver and sputter.

She said, "How is Frank, Parson?"

He looked owlishly at her. Every other sane person in Heatherton was sleeping. "He's still among us," he replied, as he walked past her to put wood in the little iron stove. As he turned he enquired if she would like hot coffee. She shook her head as she said, "Can I see him?"

The preacher nodded. "Yes, but he's still wearing his bloody clothes. I got to warn you. He don't look very good."

She hesitated near the cell-room door and spoke gravely. "It's my fault. He figured to leave this morning. I tricked him into staying, otherwise he'd have been gone an' wouldn't have got shot."

The minister absorbed all this wearing an expressionless face, but he was a life-long student of people. He also happened to be married. He smiled to her. "You can't blame yourself, young lady," he replied. "It's fate, God's working. He does these things for a purpose."

She gazed briefly at the minister then without another word turned to go down the dingy little cell-room corridor.

Fred Baca was leaning on one arm when she entered the cell. He had the other arm — his right one — beneath the old army blankets he was covered with.

Buffy smiled at him as she moved toward the cot where Frank Zurdo was sleeping like a baby. Baca relaxed but kept his right hand beneath the covers until the minister arrived, then asked him if she had come alone. Only when Eli Ross nodded did the constable bring his right hand from beneath the blankets. The six-gun he had been gripping was still under there.

Buffy sank to her knees beside Frank's cot. For a fact he did look terrible. The parson had washed him but that seemed to be only a marginal improvement; his clothing was still dark with blood, he needed a shave, his colouring was not good; he seemed to Buffy Devon more nearly dead than alive. She broke into tears.

Baca and the preacher gazed at her in dead silence. The preacher at least, knew something about women, and how they would cry when, if they had been men, they would have turned the sky blue with profanity. Different sexes, like different people, reacted differently.

She held his limp hand tightly with both of her hands. When she could stifle the sobs she spoke to the minister without taking her eyes off Frank's face. "Please don't let him die, Mister Ross."

Even Fred Baca was moved by her quavery plea. He cleared his throat. "He won't die, ma'm. He's too old."

They both looked at Baca. "Only the good die young," Baca said, and eased back down; his leg was throbbing. His injured shoulder just plain hurt.

The minister pulled over the chair he had dragged from up front, settled her on it and perched on the edge of the cot. "He's doing well," he told her, speaking quietly. "If he'd been going to die he would have done it before now. I worried because he was a bloody mess when I first saw him. I'd guess he didn't lose enough blood to die." The minister looked around, found the three-legged stool and sat on it. He didn't look much better than either of his patients. He hadn't eaten lately, his face was beard-stubbled and his clothing looked as though he had slept in it, which he had.

"I keep them both washed and disinfected, young lady. The rest of it is in God's hands."

She clung to the cold, limp hand, and leaned forward in the chair. "It's my fault. I'll never forgive myself."

Preacher Ross's voice hardened. "It was not your fault."

"It was, Parson. I made him stay when he wanted to leave."

The minister sighed. "I told you — a man's fate isn't in our hands. It's in the hands of God. Look; he's sleeping like a child. His breathing is good, his colour is better'n it was. What he needs is rest and warm food."

"And a dram of whiskey now'n then," the large man in the other cot intoned solemnly.

Oddly, the parson offered no rebuke. "Whiskey has its purpose, The Lord put everything folks need on earth for their use . . . Not for their abuse. Maybe tomorrow he can have a sip of whiskey."

Baca spoke again from across the little cell, flat on his back looking straight up. "Whiskey an' beets," he said. "My grandmother made us eat lots of beets any time we cut ourselves. Beets make blood."

Again, the minister offered a delayed response. He had been raised with the identical philosophy. "Beets indeed.

This time of year they'll be hard to come by."

Frank mumbled and feebly shifted position. The preacher sprang up and leaned. The bandage was partially visible. It showed spots of bright red. He made a little clucking sound as he leaned closer and lifted a bandaged place to look beneath it. Baca and the woman were apprehensively motionless and quiet.

Eli Ross eased back as he spoke. "It's scabbing up well enough. There are places it still looks raw. Come daylight I'll soak the cloth off and use my bear grease so's the cloth won't stick." As he resumed his perch on the three-legged stool he also said, "It's encouragin' folks, but I wish he'd been shot somewhere else. A man just naturally lies on his back. That bein' the case it'll take longer to heal."

Buffy left an hour later. When the preacher returned Baca said, "She didn't look good, friend."

Eli Ross agreed. "It's drained a lot

out of her, Clary bein' murdered an' now Mister Zurdo. She blames herself for him gettin' shot."

For the first time since Frank had been brought in and placed on the cot, Fred Baca said what he had thought after learning what had happened. "Preacher, no one with a lick of sense corners rats without makin' dead-sure all their fangs an' claws is pulled."

Eli Ross did not reply. He leaned to make a closer examination of the back-wound and tiredly straightened up. "I'll go home now," he told the marshal. "I'll be back first thing in the morning."

"Lock the damned roadway door," Baca said, "an' don't give the key to no one. I got a gun under my blankets but it only holds six slugs. Good night, preacher."

The parson did as Baca had said, he locked the jailhouse from outside. The town was now dark. His footsteps echoed as he trudged in the direction of his residence.

His wife had a fire going and one lamp lighted in the kitchen. She was a grey, plain woman with intelligent and tolerant eyes. She handed her husband a cup of coffee as he told her what he wished, what he hoped and had prayed for.

The night was very still, temperatures had dropped, the atmosphere was one of waiting. This time of year and a little later, storms came, often accompanied with driving snow.

She told her husband she had been one of the women in front of Lewis's store when Erskine had shot the rangeman and had then fired in the direction of the store.

He nodded, sipped coffee, and cocked his head slightly. It was late, close to one o'clock, he had to be mistaken but when his wife straightened up listening too, his doubts vanished.

There were horsemen out in the night. They were riding southward as though they had reached town from the north, and they were walking their horses, probably to make as little noise as possible.

Eli Ross handed his wife the coffee cup, went through to the parlour where light did not background him, and pulled aside a lace curtain. There were four of them, bundled to their gullets with their hats tipped low. He could see butt plates rising from saddle boots. His wife came silently to lean beside him. She said, "Rangemen, Eli."

He nodded. "I'm going back to the jailhouse."

She did not try to dissuade him and after he had left by the back-alley door, she remained standing in the middle of the kitchen with clenched fists. Eli was not a fighting man, he was too gentle, too compassionate to be one. Moreover, although he owned a revolver he had never carried it. She knew that to be a fact; she and Eli had been married thirty-six years.

Eli did not feel the cold as he hurried down the alley, even though it had increased since he had left the jailhouse.

It was getting along toward the wee hours when nights were coldest.

He could hear the walking horses. There was no other sound. When he got down as far as the alley-way back door of the jailhouse he was slightly breathless. The walking horses were still no farther south than the leather works.

He darted around front, unlocked the jailhouse door with fumbling fingers, stepped inside, barred the door from the inside, leaned a moment listening to his heartbeat, which seemed very loud as he listened. He could no longer hear the walking horses, but they would be out front directly.

He groped in darkness down to the cell containing the two wounded men, shook Fred Baca awake and told him what he had heard. Baca's right hand slid beneath the blankets as he hoisted himself on his good arm. "How many?"

"Four."

"Cattlemen?"

" . . . They have booted carbines. Who else could it be?"

Baca agreed. "All right. Is the door barred?"

"Yes . . . The only way they can break in here to free Mister Hendrick an' the others will be to shoot the door open."

"It'll rouse the town, Parson. They won't do that."

Baca gazed across the dark cell. Frank was staring back. He had turned only his head. Baca said, "Well, Mister Zurdo, see the fun you would have missed if you'd rode out this morning."

Frank's voice was quiet and steady. "Fetch the guns in the rack up front down here. If they get inside they'll pay for it . . . Parson? Mister Baca an' I can't move. You can bring the guns."

The minister turned at a slight sound in the cell across the corridor. That rangeman with the prominent Adam's-apple was clutching the steel straps, listening to every word. Parson Ross turned back. Neither Frank nor the marshal heeded the eavesdropper, but in their adjoining cell a cold, inflectionless voice spoke.

"A preacher an' two cripples. When they get inside they'll cut your damned throats without makin' a sound."

This time there was a response; Baca raised his six-gun from beneath the covers and cocked it. The man in the adjoining cell did not utter another sound, but a cell-mate of his did. John Hendrick did not sound as vicious as his rider had sounded when he said, "Marshal, don't get yourself killed for nothin'. There's nothin' you can do — or your friend either."

Frank replied to the cowman. "You three in that little cage, old man, are like cornered rats. You can't hide from bullets. If they bust in here you'll be the first ones to go . . . Parson, fetch them guns from the wall-rack. An' any bullets you can find."

Eli Ross dragged his feet but he went after the weapons and even found several wooden cartons with shotgun slugs and handgun bullets. When he returned Fred Baca was sitting up with his swollen leg draped over the edge of the bunk. The preacher made his clucking sound as he put the weapons down. "It's healing in fine shape, Marshal," he exclaimed. "You'll start it to bleedin' again."

Baca gave a predictable reply, one to be expected from a man of his character. "Damned if I'm goin' to lie here an' get shot in a bed. Hand me that sawed-off scattergun."

Hendrick's other rangeman, the one who had shown sense in the office yesterday, said, "Marshal, you fire one round and they'll riddle you. You'n your friend are sittin' ducks."

"One round will be all it'll take, cowboy. You'n your friends won't get out of town. Folks are already fired up; you'n your rescuers will get made into mincemeat."

The caged stockmen became silent. The pair of demoralised men across the corridor sat slumped on their bunks.

Baca methodically worked the firing mechanism of several guns, made sure they were loaded, plugged two pellet-charged casings into the short-barreled shotgun, looked over where Frank was watching and said, "First sound from out front at the door an' I'm goin' to splatter that big old man lookin' through at us, all over the wall."

Parson Ross stepped to the dingy corridor and cocked his head. He went part way toward the office to be sure, then returned. "Someone's scratchin' around the roadside door."

Frank scowled: The back-alley door was un-barred. He told the preacher to go bar it. After Eli Ross had left Frank looked at Baca. "They're crazy. Makin' noise out front sure as hell will rouse someone . . . I'd use the alley door."

Eli Ross returned. He had barred the door, but he looked puzzled. "They could have just kicked that door open an' walked in."

Baca snorted. "Nobody with a lick of sense ever said rangemen had the brains gawd give a goose . . . Are they still out front, Parson?"

The preacher went all the way up to the dark office this time. He listened and returned scowling. "They're still out there. I heard some talking, but they wasn't talkin' loud enough to make the words out through the door."

That belligerent cowboy in Hendrick's cell made one of his grisly comments. "All they got to do is slip a long knife through where the door meets the jam an' lift."

Neither the minister nor the wounded men replied. Baca strained to hear but heard nothing. He told the preacher to return to the office, watch for a knife to come in under the *tranca* and hit it as hard as he could when he saw it.

Eli Ross returned to the dark office. There was no knife showing inside. He looked for something to strike it with when it appeared. He had to settle on a hexagonal old buffalo gun with a cracked stock. The barrel was heavy. When old-timers used those big-bored guns they either had to have their victim in sight so that when they raised the rifle to their shoulders they could aim and fire in one movement, or they had to find a tree and make a hand-rest. Those old guns began to droop if a man took his time before shooting. Their accuracy was excellent, their killing-power was unsurpassed, but their barrels were solid steel and very heavy.

Parson Ross took a position on the south side of the door and waited. He held the old gun in both hands the way a man might hold a crow bar or a splitting maul.

The noise continued out front but no knife blade appeared inside the jailhouse office.

He heard voices again, was unable to distinguish words, was tempted to ease back as far as the only front-wall window and look out. The reason he did not do that was because he did not want to be distracted when the knife blade appeared.

But it did not appear. He grounded the heavy old gun and leaned on it. There were still voices outside, and they were still barely audible. He thought the men speaking were being deliberately soft-spoken.

The noise out front stopped. Parson Ross hoisted his old gun, this time letting it rest across his shoulder where the weight would not bother him as much.

It was a long wait. Cold was creeping into the jailhouse, Eli Ross had been tired before he had returned. Now, with the threatening sounds gone, he stepped back as far as the desk-chair and sank down holding the heavy old gun between his knees. He had been fearful for several hours; fear like most other human responses, was not a self-sustaining emotion unless it was fed. With no more noise out front, Parson Ross had to rouse himself with an effort. He left the old gun behind, returned to the cell and told Baca and Frank whoever had been out there was no longer making noise.

They were puzzled. They were also apprehensive. Regardless of Fred Baca's low opinion of rangemen, they were not all dense.

The irritating Hendrick-rider in the adjoining cell laughed. "You sure ain't very smart. You figured they'd blow that door open? Naw; but I'll tell you what they can do without makin' much noise: Fix two or three lass ropes to the door and gig their horses. The door'll come out."

Baca was contemptuous. "You think that wouldn't rouse the town? Mister, you're almost as dumb as you look."

Nevertheless the parson returned to the office and this time went to the little barred front window. There were no riders out there trailing lass ropes to the door. In fact there were no horsemen out there at all.

9

The Longest Night

FRANK and the marshal were incredulous. From what the minister had said there should have been men out front. That antagonistic rangeman across the corridor said, "They'll be back. Just you wait."

Frank, who had never cottoned to the rangeman, replied in a growl. "Next time you open your mouth I'm goin' to give you a third eye."

The old cowman also growled at the rangeman. "Leave it be!"

The cold was increasing, the lantern in the corridor was smoking and no one moved to turn the wick down. Parson Ross slumped in the chair Buffy Devon had used last. He was tired to the bone. A jolt of whiskey might have helped but in the parson's world liquor of any kind was the devil's brew.

Fred Baca grunted as he worked himself into a sitting position. In the poor light except for his eyes he seemed more dead than alive. He made a cold grin in Frank's direction. "The whole blessed town can't be asleep. Someone must have seen them stockmen come down here."

Frank did not reply. He had a loaded shotgun lying across his body. When he had first come around every deep breath caused pain in his upper back. Now, with the cold as well as the passage of several hours, the pain was only there when he moved, it no longer surfaced when he took down a deep breath.

"Crazy damned idiot," he muttered. The marshal looked enquiringly through the gloom. "Who?"

"Me!"

Baca solemnly nodded. "All right. Tell me something; can you roll over onto your side?"

Frank did not make the attempt. "I'll

let you know when they come down into the cell room."

John Hendrick was slumped on the wall-bunk in the adjoining cell. One of his riders was asleep on the floor, the other one rarely moved his gaze from the wounded men in the adjoining cell; no question about it, he was a vengeful, dangerous man. Frank and Baca ignored him. Baca's wounded leg throbbed with each heartbeat but the pain was more like an ache. He nevertheless only moved the leg when he had to. His shoulder wound was superficial, but it had bled enough to make his shirt soggy-stiff in back as well as in front.

Frank forced a grin as he looked at the marshal. "If either one of us ever tells folks about this night we're goin' to get laughed out of the country. Two warmed-over corpses an' a Bible banger holed up with cowmen who'd kill us in a minute if they could, and some more outside figurin' ways to get inside without rousin' the damned town."

Baca may have had a reply but before he could utter it a woman's scream from out front made everyone who heard it inside the jailhouse and elsewhere have the hair on the back of their necks stand straight up. She screamed twice.

None of the men in the cell room moved nor made a sound until Parson Ross awakened during the second scream and jolted straight up in his chair with his heart beating erratically.

He arose, ignored the handgun Fred Baca offered as he went out into the corridor and walked up to the front office. It was dark, that smoking overhead lamp had snuffed itself out.

Parson Ross went to the little barred front window and leaned hard but could see nothing, no woman, no horsemen, not even any lights, not at first anyway, but as he was leaning back someone who had been jolted awake by the scream lighted a lamp up near the saloon northward on the opposite side of Front Street.

Another lamp flickered to light, then several others. On a dead-still night that woman's scream had reached through town in a way a normal daytime shout never would have.

Eli Ross stepped to the door, leaned and listened. There was not a sound until he was startled by someone banging on the back-alley door.

He remained in place until it appeared that cowmen would not be doing that, it had to be someone from town. He went back there and called, "Who is it? What do you want?"

The answer came in a nearly frantic breathlessness. "It's Buffy. Let me in. Please let me in!"

"Who is with you?" Eli Ross asked.

Her reply was sharper, more nearly hysterical. "No one. I'm alone. Is that you Parson?" The near-hysteria was becoming increasingly noticeable. "Please! Let me in!"

He lifted the bar, uttered a short prayer and opened the door. She shot past him, did not stop until she was in the office. When he joined her after re-barring the alley-way door she was standing in the middle of the room with her back to him and both hands to her mouth. In the poor light she looked frightened out of her wits. She pointed to the door as she spoke through her fingers. "He's dead, Parson. Open the door . . . He's dead."

The preacher was badly upset. He made no move to open the roadway door. "Buffy, set down, get hold of yourself."

She did not move. "They hung him from the upper jamb of the doorway, Parson . . . I couldn't sleep . . . I wanted to come up here and help . . . He was hanging there. It was terrible . . . I screamed."

Parson Ross considered the woman a moment longer then returned to the recessed barred little front window. Try as he might he could not see around the wall to the doorway.

When he turned Buffy was shaking. He helped her sit down and did what his wife never would have approved of, he fumbled until he found the whiskey bottle, splashed a little into a tin cup, handed it to her and said, "Hold your breath and drink this."

She obeyed, and immediately arched forward coughing.

From the cell room Fred Baca yelled. "Preacher! What in hell's goin' on up there? Is there a woman up there?"

Eli Ross did not answer, he had his back to the ajar cell room door as he patted Buffy's back. It was the only thing he could think to do.

The next voice from the cells belonged to Frank Zurdo. "Is that Buffy? Parson, damn you, *answer me!*"

"It's Buffy," Ross called back. "I let her in the back door."

"What was she yellin' about?"

"She wants me to open the roadway door. She says there's someone hangin' out there."

Not another word came from the cell room. The minister got Buffy sitting up straight. He got her a cup of water which she drank with tears streaming down both cheeks. When she handed back the cup she looked up. She no longer shook, her gaze was still fixed, the pupils distended until her eyes seemed almost black, but her voice was steady.

"Ed Erskine is hanging in the doorway out front."

Parson Ross put the cup aside without speaking for a long time, not until Frank yelled again. "What did she say?"

"She said Ed Erskine's hangin' in the jailhouse doorway out front."

Fred Baca bellowed. "Open the damned door a crack. Cock a gun an' point it through."

Eli Ross had no weapon, nor did he approach the door. There was a splinter of dawn-light showing off in the sooty east.

"Parson! Did you open the door?" Baca bellowed.

Eli Ross approached the door,

hesitated before reaching for the tranca, and looked back. Buffy was staring at him; she looked ghost-like. Ross raised the bar slowly and soundlessly. His heart was pounding. He raised the bar from off its hangers, opened the door a crack, stood as though he'd turned to stone for a long moment, then closed the door and replaced the tranca. Without a glance at the woman or a word he went down to the cells where Frank, the marshal and the cowmen were staring.

"It's Erskine. He's hanging in the doorway out front. He's dead."

Baca growled. "You sure?"

The minister stared at the big man with the swollen leg and torn, blood-caked clothing. "I'm sure. His head is too far to one side. His neck is broke."

Baca eased his back against the wall of his bunk. Frank gritted his teeth and eased over on his side where he could see the minister better. He had the shotgun at his side on the bunk.

"They caught him. Parson, you know the name of the fellers who went after him?"

Ross tiredly wagged his head. "No, but I expect folks around town will know who they were."

Baca broke into this discussion. "Let me tell you two gents somethin'. The son of a bitch is dead. He had it comin' in spades. As long as I'm lawman here, they can cut him down come daylight, bury the son of a bitch and that will end it . . . No questions asked, no nosin' around."

Preacher Ross gazed at the big man whose dark beard-stubbled face lent him the appearance of an old-time pirate. Baca thought the minister was going to speak, maybe protest, so he held up a thick finger and wagged it. "Nothin', Preacher. Not a gawddamned word."

Frank twisted to look in the adjoining cell where big old John Hendrick was standing like a statue. That disagreeable rangeman was slumped on the bunk considering his boots. Even the milder of the three who had been roused from his sleep by the racket up front, seemed to have lost the ability to speak.

Frank addressed the cowman. "If you paid him in advance to kill me, you lost your damned money, old man."

Hendrick did not respond.

Buffy appeared in the sickly predawn light. She had good colour which was not noticeable in the gloom, and her eyes were bright. "I . . . there wasn't anyone out there when I came along . . . Whoever put him up there was gone. But a livery animal a townsman got from me last night was back in the corral. He'd been rode hard. So had the other horse . . . The one Ed took."

Fred Baca growled. "That's enough, ma'm. Folks can bury him an' since I'm the law here I say that ends it."

There was no way to misinterpret Baca's meaning; he neither wanted to know who had caught and lynched Erskine, nor what folks speculated about on the subject. Frank, gazing at the big man with the swollen leg and the dark, hard gaze, thought he understood Fred Baca better than he expected to. Baca operated according to range law exactly as most men did west of the Missouri River. That would eventually change, but when it did the change would not be for the better. Book-law in the view of most rangemen had very little to do with justice.

Parson Ross took the basin of cold pink water to fling it out back and return with a fresh basin-full of water. As he set the basin down he looked from Baca to Zurdo. "I don't know where to begin . . . Buffy, I'd take it kindly if you'd go ask my wife for a full bottle of carbolic acid an' another cake of soap along with clean rags for bandages." When she made no move to depart Frank said, "Let her out the alley door, Preacher."

The sun came; at first light filtered through soot, but that did not last long. When it climbed high enough to be clear of earth's atmosphere it shone brightly and, eventually, warmly. It was going to be another of those rare golden days of autumn, the one called Indian summer.

The cowman who was clearly visible in the adjoining cell of Baca and Zurdo was sitting slumped gazing at the floor. His cellmates were also relaxed and silent, but the hard eyes of the dogged rangeman were fixed on Frank. His temperament had not changed since he'd been disarmed and locked up. It would never change; he was a product of his time. His breed of men had one particular virtue: Loyalty. It went with the brand they rode for, with the men they worked with, otherwise they were unyielding individuals whose existence centred around what they perceived as good and evil, right and wrong; very often the distinction was personal and had nothing to do with the values and principles of others.

Parson Ross soaked Baca's bandage

until it could be peeled off. There was no sign of infection, which was a miracle, but the bullet holes through the leg were purplish and swollen. The preacher put off re-bandaging the leg until Buffy returned. While the preacher was working on his patients someone out front let out a bawling yelp. The town was about to see the grisly 'thing' with the broken neck hanging utterly still in front of the jailhouse door.

Parson Ross was working on Frank, who was lying on his stomach, when some outraged soul hammered on the roadside door. Fred Baca eased to the edge of his bunk to stand up but the preacher stopped him. "I'll see who it is."

The visitor was not alone. There were several men out front but the two who had shoved the dangling corpse away so they could knock on the door were the beanpole from the leather works and the stocky, bull-necked stager with the trimmed grey beard and short temper.

As they considered the preacher the stager turned and growled at the men behind him. "Take the son of a bitch down."

He and the harness-maker entered, the stager closed the roadway door at his back. Parson Ross told them about the nightlong vigil. The burly, shorter man wanted to know who-all was in the cells. When Eli Ross told him, the stager grunted. "There's a lynchin' party waitin' an' ready, preacher."

The minister's eyes widened. "What for, Jess? Someone already hung Ed. He was the one — "

"Preacher he was the *main* one, and them damned overbearin' cowmen put Erskine up to it, an' they was responsible for Clary Devon bein' shot in cold blood. They been ridin' roughshod over our town too long. We got plenty of rope, plenty of horses for 'em to straddle, an' we got the place picked out where to hang 'em."

The minister held fisted hands at his side as he looked from the tall man to the shorter one. "There's John Hendrick," he said. "If something happens to him rangemen will come down on this town like the devil an' his imps."

The stager was unrelenting. "Let 'em come, Eli. We'll be waitin'. This business has gone on too long as it is. They want trouble — we'll give 'em a belly full."

A noise behind Parson Ross made him turn. The two men facing him had already seen the woman supporting the man who had a shotgun in his hands. The harness-maker spoke quietly. "Mister Zurdo, I told you to be careful."

Frank replied in a husky tone of voice. "I was careful."

"No you wasn't. Men like Erskine always carry a belly-gun."

Frank did not respond. He gazed at the stager longest, but his gaze included the harness-maker. "No lynching, gents."

The stager bristled. "Them stockmen is responsible for the death of Buffy's husband. They tried to kill you. They shot up the constable. Now mister, Heatherton's had enough. We're goin' to settle this once an — "

Frank was weak, Buffy held him around the waist in a surprisingly strong grip as he raised the shotgun, aimed it squarely at the stager's soft parts. "Buffy's husband got settled for. Me'n the marshal will live. It'd be up to us, not you gents, to settle for what the stockmen did to us. You go back out there, haul Erskine away — dump him in the garbage pit for all I care, but that ends it."

Jess Ames's eyes widened in disbelief. "You want them murderin' damned cowmen to just ride out of town? Mister, Heatherton won't never allow that."

Frank was tiring fast. He drew back both hammers of the scattergun. It required considerable effort. He steadied the gun on the stager. "You're dead-set on hangin' them?"

"Yes I am. So is — "

"I'm goin' to blow you through the door."

The harness-maker squawked. "Hold it! . . . Mister Zurdo, settle down."

Frank nodded slightly. "All right. You gents come in here to use force to get the rangemen. An' I'm using force to keep you from gettin' your damned town burnt down around your ears, an' some of your townsfolk shot. Now — Mister Stager, the only way you're going back out of here alive is to pass me your word you'll stop the talk of lynching. Get 'em to unwind. Tell 'em if they lynch these men when the cowmen come to settle up, they'll wish to gawd they never seen a hang-rope . . . Well; do I get your word or not?" Frank shifted the twin steel barrels slightly so that if he fired both the men facing him would be blown to mincemeat.

The harness-maker spoke first, his

voice high and slightly scratchy; the bravest man on earth facing a double barreled shotgun from about ten or twelve feet with both hammers at full cock and the man holding the weapon with his finger inside the triggerguard, had reason to hesitate.

"I never really liked the idea," the beanpole said. "There's too many of 'em." He turned toward his companion. "I'm willin' to talk down the lynchin'. How about you, Jess?"

The burly, bearded man looked steadily at Frank. If he was afraid it did not show. He nodded his head, but he said, "It's on your head, mister, if folks can't be settled down."

"Make sure you try," Frank replied. "Come back when you think the lynchin' won't take place."

Once they were outside where townsmen waited, the harness-maker leaned to speak to his shorter companion. "He'd have done it, Jess. He ain't been here long but I've known his kind before . . . Sure as hell he'd have done it."

The stager was grim-faced as he growled for everyone to follow him up to the saloon.

10

A New Day

MOST of the irate townsmen were not up and stirring when the harness-maker addressed Henry Bolton and the straggle of citizens who had been aroused.

He explained what Frank Zurdo had said in as few words as were required, then turned toward the stager. Everyone in the room knew Jess Aymes to be a very stubborn, straightforward individual. The stager growled to Bolton for a jolt. He downed the whiskey before speaking. More townsmen were drifting in; Bolton's saloon was the traditional gathering place. It was also the only lighted business establishment the full length of Front Street.

The stager ground out each word as though it caused him physical pain. He told them basically what the harness-maker had already said. He did not say he favoured abandoning the lynching, but he did repeat what Frank had said about the consequences — stockmen would come to town from all directions armed to the gills and spoiling for a fight.

When the stager finished there was not a word except for a call to Henry for a drink here and there among the townsmen, until one man reared back from the bar to say, "Who the hell does this Zurdo feller think he is?"

The harness-maker answered shortly. "Every man-jack of you been growlin' around an' talkin' hard since Clary Devon was killed . . . An' that's all you done. Mister Zurdo come along an' Beaman got settled with. Right now he's hurt bad down in the jailhouse, an' he makes sense. The stockmen'll burn this damned town to the ground if you hang them stockmen at the jailhouse."

"Well . . . What're we supposed to do? Stand for more of their danged meanness? Somewhere we got to take a stand."

The harness-maker had no solution, neither did anyone else in the saloon, but Jess Ames said, "I'm for lynchin' them bastards — but I don't want to get burnt out. Neither do the rest of you. So — we wait a while then we palaver."

"Palaver with who?" a townsman asked. "Them damned cowmen? That'll be like beggin' an' I don't have no intention of bowin' to any damned rangemen."

"We'll palaver with Mister Zurdo," the stager said, and coldly looked around the room. "Him and the new marshal. They done what the rest of us didn't do. As far as I'm concerned they've earned the right for us to listen to 'em."

That pretty well settled the matter for the time being although there were townsmen who had remained silent at the saloon and who still favoured lynching.

The sun rose higher, warmth came with it, but not immediately. The sky was soft blue from horizon to horizon. Heatherton gradually came to life. People turned from their chores to look in the direction of the jailhouse, which was closed, forbidding looking, with a wisp of rope someone had cut hanging from the baulk above the roadway door.

Parson Ross came out eventually, nodded and headed for his cottage without pausing along the way although a number of people would have buttonholed him if they could have.

His wife was waiting but the preacher was too exhausted to talk much. He crawled into bed, asleep almost before his head touched the pillow.

For the men at the jailhouse Buffy agreed to cross to the cafe and fetch back food.

There were a few early diners but not many. The moment she walked in and asked the cafeman for buckets for the occupants of the jailhouse the questions started. She smiled a lot and avoided direct answers. Two men volunteered to help her carry the pails across the road. When they were inside she had them put the little pails on the desk then closed the door behind them. They made a bee-line for the cafe where other men were waiting.

Buffy fed the men, refused to talk to the prisoners, particularly the hard-eyed Hendrick-rider who tried to get a conversation going.

She fussed over Frank and the constable. The saloonman arrived as the sun was climbing. When Buffy opened the door to let Henry enter she had a glimpse of the staring crowd over in front of the general store. She barred the door, gestured for Bolton to enter the cell room, then hurried out into the back-alley southward to do her chores at the barn.

Down there she encountered three rangemen who had evidently been waiting for her — for someone anyway — as though they were not quite willing to go up to the store or the saloon.

One of them was a grizzled, weathered, lined individual with tufted grey eyebrows and shrewd little blue eyes. His name was Alfred Cullin. The other men were his riders. Cullin owned one of the larger outfits in the Heatherton country. Buffy had heard, without verification, that Alfred Cullin's sister had been John Hendrick's wife. She had died years earlier.

The old man was tough, hard as stone, direct and calculating. He was also gallant; his generation had been raised to be that way toward female women. He smiled at Buffy as he said, "We been waitin'. You had to come do the chores sooner or later."

She sat on the bench in front of the harness room quiet and poker-faced. The old man settled beside her. His riders slouched across the runway like crows on a fence.

Cullin was placating. "I heard about the trouble in town, young lady."

She turned. "Is that why you stayed

down here instead of going up through town?"

The old man nodded. "Didn't seem like a good idea, folks fired up an' all."

Buffy sighed as she regarded the cowman. She had known him by sight. This was the first time she had ever spoken to him. She had heard he was both wealthy and hard as nails. Right now he seemed almost gentle toward her, which did not quite square with all she'd heard, but then what folks heard about people was more often tainted by bias most would not admit to, like jealousy because the cowman was reputed to be rich, and general dislike because he was a stockman. Bias and prejudice didn't have to be reasonable.

He asked about John Hendrick. Buffy told him. She also mentioned the pair of wounded men, how they had been injured, the dangling corpse in front of the jailhouse door, the other rangemen locked in cells. She ended up by telling him the town was in a lynching mood.

Cullin was not surprised. "It wouldn't be a good idea," he told her quietly, without elaborating. He also said, he would like to get inside the jailhouse and talk to John Hendrick.

She told him frankly she would not help him get inside. He did not argue; he leaned on the bench to roll and light a smoke. As he straightened back he looked in the direction of his riders. They looked back.

Buffy arose. She had chores to do. Cullin arose to lend a hand. He and his riders knew what to do and did it. Not a word was exchanged as the work was done. Not until the men were lining up their tools did one of the riders speak to Buffy. He was young; in face he was younger than she was. They were standing slightly apart from the others when the cowboy said, "Ma'm, four of us come to town. Mister Cullin sent one of us to go among the cow outfits, sort of let 'em know what's happenin' in Heatherton." He smiled before turning to join his companions. "Just between you'n me, Mister Cullin might not like me warnin' you."

Buffy wanted to return to the jailhouse. As far as she knew the preacher hadn't returned, and the men in there she cared about were about as close to being helpless as men could be.

Alfred Cullin was a deliberate individual. He sat on the bench out front of the harness room smoking and thoughtful. When Buffy approached he said, "I heard about your husband. I'm real sorry."

She stopped in front of him. "I don't want to talk about that, Mister Cullin."

He nodded with understanding, then changed the subject. "Seems to me, young lady, between the two us we got to stop what's coming."

"What's coming, Mister Cullin?" she asked with a challenging stare. "More stockmen and their riders?"

He leaned his back against rough wood behind the bench. "This time of year stockmen don't have many riders, just the ones they keep to winter feed."

She thought that was an evasion so she said, "So they'll come anyway?"

He turned, considered her for a moment then smiled a little. "You'd like my wife; you'n her are alike. She's sort of snippy an' hard-headed too." His smile lingered. "What'll it take to get you to help me get inside the jailhouse?" Before she could reply Cullin held up a hand. "I'll go alone an unarmed. I just want to hear what John Hendrick's got to say . . . Ma'm, trouble's comin' as sure as we're sittin' here. I'd like to head it off if I can."

She glanced in the direction of the youngest cowboy. He almost imperceptibly nodded his head.

Buffy understood the mood of the town; all it would take to start a shooting war would be for rangemen to converge in numbers on Heatherton.

She sat a long moment struggling to make a decision. Of one thing she was certain; Frank and the marshal needed better care in cleaner surroundings than they would get in the jailhouse. She also wanted to trust the older man with the thin but seemingly genuine smile. In the end, if he went in unarmed and alone . . .

She said, "You leave your gun on the bench and your riders stay here."

Cullin leaned to put his gun on the bench, straightened around to shake his head at his riders and followed Buffy out into the back alley where they walked side by side in the direction of the jailhouse, were about half way along when a large brindle dog lunged at them through a tumble-down fence. He was wearing a collar to which was attached a chain.

It startled Buffy, she recoiled against the older man who would not have stopped if she hadn't. He pointed a finger and said, "Lem, you get back in your yard an' shut up or I'm goin' to stomp half the waddin' out of you!"

The dog stopped struggling to reach the people.

Cullin leaned to pick up a rock, of which there were none, and the dog yelped and disappeared back through the old fence.

Cullin shook his head. "He belongs to an old man who used to ride for my paw years back. Every blessed time I come by to see his owner he makes out like he's goin' to chew me up . . . I've known Lem since he was a pup; he still acts like he's goin' to eat me alive . . . Come along. He won't come back."

Buffy was wary but the big dog did not re-appear. They were at the rear door of the jailhouse when she looked at the cowman. "Do you carry a belly-gun, Mister Cullin?"

He looked more hurt than surprised. "I never carried one in my life."

"I had to ask. That's what Ed Erskine shot Frank Zurdo with across the back in front of the jailhouse."

He stood a moment without reaching for the latch of the door as he said, "Who hung Erskine?"

"I don't know, Mister Cullin, and if I did I wouldn't tell you."

Inside, she led the way through to the office after barring the alley door. She was committed to bringing Cullin into the jailhouse, but no one else. She thought he could be trusted — still — he was a stockman; right now stockmen were anathema to Buffy Devon and the rest of Heatherton.

The cowman wrinkled his nose. "Smells like a pig pen in here."

She took him down into the cell room where every eye stared at them. She told Frank and the marshal who he was, the others required no introduction. They started to speak until Cullin held up a hand, went to the front of the cell containing Hendrick and asked a question. "John — what in hell got into you?"

Hendrick looked at the shorter, slighter man. "That feller with the bloody leg — he's the one who killed Sage. I lost more'n Sage in that fight at the saloon."

Alfred Cullin waited until that had been said. His gaze into the cell was not as much unfriendly as it was critical. "Beaman's no loss," he told the other older man, who was a head taller than Alfred Cullin. "How come Ed Erskine to be in town? Last I heard he was back-shootin' sheep herders in Wyoming?"

Hendrick neither answered nor looked Cullin in the eye. Behind him that hard-eyed rangeman spoke. "Mister Cullin, the town was spoilin' for trouble. All us fellers wanted to do was ride in, have a few drinks, maybe play cards, then leave."

Fred Baca growled from the adjoining cell. "You lyin' bastard."

Cullin turned. He had heard Heatherton had hired a new town marshal but this was the first time he'd seen him. Cullin said, "That leg looks pretty bad, mister."

"It feels bad," Baca replied, and glared at the men in the adjoining cell. "They was loaded for bear. I went into the saloon — the fight started. I nailed Beaman. Everyone was shootin' when Mister Zurdo here bought in. There was two left when the smoke cleared ... Them two in the cell behind you."

Cullin did not look around, he shifted his gaze to Frank but said nothing until he'd finished his cursory inspection of the second wounded man in soiled clothing whose bandage showed blood. He faced John Hendrick again and wagged his head. "John, I told my sister before she married you that you was a good stockman but otherwise a damned fool ... I know you John. How did Erskine happen to be down here?"

The antagonistic rangeman with the hard eyes spoke. "I sent for him."

Cullin's tufted eyebrows shot up. "You? Who are you?"

Hendrick answered defensively. "His

name's Sam Owen, he's been my top hand. He signed on to winter feed."

Cullin eyed the hard-eyed man. "Sam Owen. John, did you get this rider of yours to send for Erskine?"

For three seconds the only sound inside the cell room was Heatherton's noises outside. Cullin sighed and wagged his head again. "John, you really are a damned fool. From what I've figured — you pushed for this mess. It's a wonder to me they ain't lynched you by now."

Frank spoke for the first time. "It's in the air, Mister Cullin. I told a couple of 'em if they tried it the sky would fall on 'em. Right now we're waitin'. Just waitin', but all I wanted to do was ride through Heatherton on my way out of snow country, an' I'd like to know whether they're comin' back to hang your friends. If they are, then it'll delay me another few days. If they aren't, I'd like to saddle up an' — "

"Frank," Buffy exclaimed, "you

wouldn't get a mile down the road in your shape."

Cullin looked from Frank to the woman, then said, "I'd as soon not be in here if a mob of lynchers comes." He turned finally and glanced at the pair of men in the cell across the corridor. He said nothing to them and they said nothing either.

Buffy broke the silence. "Mister Cullin; did you send for more stockmen?"

He eyed her a moment before answering. "Yes'm. The reason was because I only knew there was ranchers and their riders locked up here after there'd been a fight."

Another silence followed those words.

Fred Baca ran a hand across his stubbly jaw as he eyed Alfred Cullin. "Mister, I think you'd better stay in the jailhouse with us."

Cullin's reply was short. "No, I don't think so. Right now I think what I got to do is go out a ways an' stop the riders before they get here."

Frank asked if Cullin thought he could do that. The older man wasn't sure. "I got two men with me. Between the three of us we can maybe stop most of 'em."

Cullin turned back to face John Hendrick again. He didn't speak, he just stood gazing in at the larger man before he turned toward Buffy. "Bar that alley door after me, ma'm."

Fred Baca clearly wanted to keep Cullin as a hostage but without support he gloweringly watched the wiry older man follow Buffy.

That mild-mannered rider in Hendrick's cell stood beneath the high, very narrow barred window of his cell and remarked to the others, who were not interested, that the jailhouse was beginning to smell like a buzzard's breath.

When Buffy returned she brought two pails of water. Frank and Fred Baca drank first then tried to clean up. While they were doing this the minister returned. He looked clean and refreshed. He told Buffy his wife would like her to come up yonder where there was soap, water, and out back a zinc bathing tub.

Buffy went. Parson Ross examined his patients, washed them, scrubbed hard enough to earn groans, and made fresh bandages. When he was finished the predominant smell was of lye soap and carbolic acid.

They told him about Cullin's visit. He listened then told them something they hadn't known.

"When I first came here Mister Cullin was the town marshal. That's been eighteen, maybe twenty years back. His sister was alive then." Eli Ross did not look at John Hendrick as he said this. "She could coax a bird down out of a tree. Her'n my missus was close friends. When she died my missus was bad off for a month."

From the adjoining cell John Hendrick said, "Shut up, Eli."

The preacher regarded Hendrick for a moment or two, then turned his back and talked about other things.

11

A Gathering Storm

HEATHERTON would have enjoyed the unseasonal warmth more if it hadn't had other things to worry about. For example, word had spread through town that rangemen had been seen leaving town at the lower end, which worried folks because it meant they had been in town unbeknownst and this was a source for fresh anxiety.

Those favouring lynching began to harangue less about it. At Bolton's saloon there were glum customers whose earlier anger and ardour had been reduced to grumbling and indecision.

For Alfred Cullin and his riders the plan was simple; each man would select one of the customary routes used by stockmen coming to town, stop the riders who had been told of trouble and try to get them to either meet Alfred Cullin at the livery barn without riding through town to get down there, or to simply turn back.

Neither Cullin nor his riders thought the stockmen would turn back, and they were right. The issue of the stockmen versus townsmen had been simmering too long. They knew of the fight at the saloon and how it had ended.

Henry Bolton came down to the jailhouse to palaver. He told Frank and the marshal that there was a rumour stockmen were coming in force to free the prisoners.

No one denied the rumour but Fred Baca surprised Frank and the preacher when he explained what Alfred Cullin was going to try, and said he hoped wholeheartedly Cullin was successful.

This departure from the wounded lawman's earlier attitude of fire and brimstone encouraged John Hendrick to say, "Al Cullin's got influence with the ranchers."

Baca snarled at the other large man in the adjoining cell. You aren't leavin'. The others can go, if that's how folks want it, but not you."

Buffy returned with pails from the cafe and a note from the preacher's wife, which Eli read twice, then addressed the others. "There's some cowmen palaverin' west of town. My wife saw 'em through my spyglass. She couldn't make them out, it was too far, but she wrote they're settin' out there like In'ians at a powwow."

Hendrick said, "From the west? That'll be my neighbors from the Brody place an' most likely from the Dugan an' Cowley outfits."

No one commented. In fact no one even looked at the prisoner.

Frank's back was painful but it no longer bled if he moved with care and caution. He could sit on the edge of the bunk and as long as he avoided twisting there was more itch than pain. He and Baca exchanged a glance. The marshal said, "I owe you, Mister Zurdo."

Frank nodded. "All right, Marshal. When this is over you can pay me off with a bottle of bonded whiskey."

Henry Bolton's eyes widened. "Frank, there ain't been a bottle of bonded whiskey in this town since I been here."

Zurdo's reply was short. "I didn't say he had to pay me back in Heatherton. I was thinkin' more like some place with a Mex name down south."

Buffy left the cell room and returned with a basin of hot water and two clean rags. She put the basin on the chair, looped one of the clean cloths around Frank's gullet and produced an ivory-handled straight razor.

Every man watched as she soaped Frank's face, hooked her arms high, turned his face by the nose and went to work.

Baca lighted one half of a cigar. The other half remained in his pocket; somewhere over the last day or so the cigar had been broken. The fragrance was pleasant. Eli Ross slipped up to the front office, found the whiskey bottle, held it at arm's length as though he were gripping a rattlesnake, and returned to the cell room. Baca took the first two swallows. The bottle went around from Henry Bolton to Frank, to Baca again, and to Buffy, who poured some into the basin and rinsed Frank's face with the laced water when she finished shaving him.

She stood back eyeing her handiwork. Frank smiled. "I'm obliged. It don't itch any more."

She turned toward Fred Baca. He eyed the razor and shook his head. "I'm growin' a beard," he told her in a very serious tone of voice. Only two prisoners did not laugh, they were John Hendrick and the hard-eyed rangeman called Sam Owen.

Henry left. Out front of the jailhouse he was met by Wes Hamilton and Jess Ames who had been about to knock when Henry opened the door.

"They're comin'," the stager said,

and gestured with a powerful arm. "Looks like maybe twelve, fifteen of 'em. From the east." Ames lowered his arm, waiting for the saloonman's reaction.

Henry was not really surprised, but he'd had other things on his mind and could only stand there until the beanpole harness-maker spoke. "Folks been gatherin' over at the store."

Bolton nodded and led the way. Up to this point Heatherton's residents were pretty much of one mind; they were almost unanimously antagonistic toward stockmen and, justified or not, were in a troublesome mood, but that was pretty much the extent of their antagonism; they were not entirely prepared for a genuine battle, something they now expected since the stockmen were converging on their town. It was one thing to make threats and something altogether different to see armed men approaching as a result of those threats.

The women particularly, were

unresolved. Their warnings and fears were transmitted to the men. Jess Ames the stager listened and shook his head. When he and his companions entered the store the argument was going on full force.

He took the harness-maker and the saloonman to one side to say, "This ain't goin' to work. Look at 'em. Listen to 'em. If there's goin' to be a fight folks got to be of one mind. Look around; there's gettin' to be less an' less fight an' more confusion . . . Where the hell is all the resolve folks had a couple weeks back?"

Henry said nothing, neither did the harness-maker. They watched the crowd, listened to the arguing, looked at one another and the saloonman spoke to the stager. "Like a lot of chickens . . . We better go see where them stockmen are."

They left the general store. Although it was a day of autumn gold when people would ordinarily have been outside, the sidewalks on both sides of Front Street had very few pedestrians using them.

Jess Ames, whose yard was at the north end of town, left his companions out front of the saloon. If trouble came from the north he had more to lose.

When he walked to the rear of his yard he saw horsemen approaching at a walk from the west. He watched for a while then went out front. There were more riders coming from the northeast, also at a slow walk.

Someone yelled from southward, down in the direction of the livery barn. Jess turned, saw a man he thought was a rider down there standing wide-legged in front of the barn. He watched and wondered; the rangeman had to be a damned fool to expose himself like that in a hostile town — except that the stager was no longer so sure the town was hostile.

The rangeman sauntered out of sight inside the livery barn.

Jess wasn't the only person who heard that yell, people appeared at windows and in doorways. The preacher cracked the roadway door of the jailhouse and joined others in seeking the significance of that yell.

Behind him in the cell-room a man laughed derisively. As the preacher was barring the door he heard the same man say, "Marshal, if you're a prayin' man you better start. Cullin ain't goin' to stop anyone."

Baca did not bother to reply. His leg was itching, the swelling had decreased, the parson's care seemed to have worked well enough.

Buffy went up to the office to get rid of her basin full of water when someone rapped with a gun butt on the roadway door.

She put the basin on the desk and leaned as she asked who was out there. The answer she got was in a recognisable voice. "Al Cullin, ma'm."

She opened the door. As the wiry older man entered he tugged off his gloves, nodded and marched past on his way into the cellroom. He ignored the prisoners as he said, "I done as well as I could. Some of them are down at the livery barn. They'll talk." Cullin was unsmiling as he also said, "One of my riders went after Everett Lewis, the storekeeper, another went after Henry Bolton and whoever else he can corral to come down and talk. I told 'em about you gents; they'd like to palaver with you too, but I told 'em can't neither of you walk that far." Cullin looked at John Hendrick from an expressionless face, then turned on his heel as he asked Buffy to let him out and to bar the door after him.

Frank stroked his smooth face which smelled of whiskey. Baca had his swollen leg straight out on his bunk. He blew out a sigh. "I been in bad spots before," he told no one in particular, "but this one takes the blue ribbon." He paused a moment before also saying, "If Mister Cullin hadn't come along we might have been a lot worse off . . . Us and the town both."

Buffy went after two more buckets

of water. The sun was climbing and while it was pleasant outside, inside it got downright hot.

Jess Ames appeared at the jailhouse. He told them what he had seen, groups of rangemen near the upper end of town. They told him about Cullin and he left to go to the lower end of town too.

Buffy and the minister went to the cafe for more of those little pails of stew and black coffee. On their way back they saw rangemen lounging in sunlight out front of her barn. The preacher thought he recognised several of those men but Buffy could name every one as well as the outfits they rode for.

They had just barely had time to distribute the food when someone hammered on the roadside door. Alfred Cullin had the results of the palaver at the lower end of town. He did not look cheerful as he said, "They want all the prisoners set loose. They also want the man who killed Sage Beaman.

An' one other thing — they want one of their riders to take the job of town marshal."

No one said a word, only the disagreeable man in Hendrick's cell, Sam Owen, smiled.

Fred Baca looked steadily at Alfred Cullin. "Did you pitch in with 'em?"

Cullin reddened. "No, I didn't pitch in with 'em, you danged outlander."

"You know damned well we can't agree to them terms," the marshal exclaimed.

Frank interrupted. "Mister Cullin, you can tell 'em they can have the man who killed Beaman any time they want to walk up here one at a time, an' open the door. He an' I'll be waiting. As for the rest of it, go get your answers from the folks at the general store. It's up to them . . . One more thing, Mister Cullin: If they want to come up here Mister Baca an' I'll be glad to explain things."

Alfred Cullin nodded without speaking. He'd had a fair idea something like this was going to be the reply he was to carry back to the livery barn.

Baca asked, "How many are there?"

Cullin answered curtly, "Fifteen with more comin'. Don't make a fight out of it. If you do they'll bury you an' torch the town."

After Cullin had left there was very little said. Except for that smug rangeman named Owen spirits were low. John Hendrick had figured out that no matter how this ended he was not going to emerge smelling of roses. After a few attempts by the hard-eyed rider to engage Hendrick in conversation without getting so much as a grunt, Owen joined the others in silence.

Buffy took the preacher up front and closed the door so they could not be heard in the cell-room. "I'm going over to the store," she told the minister. "Folks aren't going to like what the cattlemen want. If they're divided now, after they hear what Mister Cullin said I'll gamble it'll get them mad all over again, especially that business of the ranchers wanting one of their men appointed marshal."

She was right; when she told her story across Front Street the indecision vanished. Even Jess Ames and the harness-maker were surprised by the abrupt change. They were also heartened by it.

A townsman loudly demanded that every man get weapons and follow him down the alley on the east side. They would appear across from the livery barn armed, ready to fight, and in numbers more than enough to make the cowmen think twice.

Wes Hamilton rolled his eyes. "Don't do no such a thing. What we need is to break them stockmen to lead without gettin' folks killed."

"How?" demanded the loud-mouthed townsman.

"For one thing we wait until they've heard what Cullin says. If they scoff at what the fellers at the jailhouse said, why then some of us — more'n they got — walk down there unarmed and give 'em a choice. Start trouble an' we'll hang every cowman in the jailhouse — then — if they want a fight, we'll smoke 'em out . . . Only first, one thing at a time."

Hamilton's logic soaked in gradually, but about half the people in the general store were fired up to fight. When they growled the storekeeper, who had up until now remained in the background, spoke without raising his voice. "Any way you look at it, whether we run them off or they run us to cover, the town's goin' to be bad off — maybe burnt to the ground. I sure as hell don't want that. I got a lot of money in my store and my inventory. The rest of you . . . You got houses or businesses . . . It won't hurt to do like Wes says: Wait until things is clearer."

Buffy and the widow-woman named Alicia Hovencroft, the local seamstress, exchanged a smile. There were more men than women in the store but they took their cue from the livery-lady and the seamstress, they also smiled.

The beanpole went out front with Buffy; while gazing over at the jailhouse he said, "You got a clean rag over there?" She nodded. "Fine. Now then, when Mister Cullin comes back with the answer, if it's decent, we'll wait for you to come back to the store. If it ain't decent, if they want a fight, you hang a white cloth in the front window."

She nodded and held out her hand. She and the older man shook solidly. He watched her cross the road. Southward near the lower end of town, others also watched her leave the store heading for the jailhouse. Alfred Cullin was among them. He said something to the lounging rangemen before starting up the plankwalk.

Although Front Street was empty — there was not even a saddle animal at the tie-racks — townsfolk watched from dozens of windows and recessed doorways.

The men in the jailhouse listened carefully as Buffy explained what had been said across the road. When she finished there was a long silence before Fred Baca said, "It won't end well; both sides is too far apart."

Before more could be said Cullin hammered on the roadway door with his gun butt. The preacher admitted him, took one look at the cowman's face and decided the marshal had been right.

Cullin stopped in front of the cell where Frank and the marshal were. He completely ignored the others. "They'll leave off havin' one of their men serve as town marshal, but they want the man who killed Sage Beaman, an' they want him brought down to the livery barn by the prisoners . . . Every prisoner set loose."

Silence settled. That mild-mannered rangeman in Hendrick's cell broke it by noisily drinking water.

Eli Ross spoke quietly. "Mister Cullin, would it do any good if I went down an' talked to them?"

The weathered stockman eyed the

preacher for a long moment before wagging his head without speaking.

Frank asked if Cullin had told the stockmen if they wanted Beaman's killer they could come get him — and Frank — any time they cared to try it.

Cullin eyed the speaker, who had a clean face but otherwise looked like something a tanyard pup might have dragged in. "I told 'em, Mister Zurdo. They want the marshal . . . Maybe you too, but mostly they want the marshal." Cullin paused. "Some more fellers rode in."

"How many?" Baca asked.

"All together, there's twenty-six now."

Buffy went to the front window of the office, stood where she could be seen and shook her head. She was unable to tell whether they had seen her across the road because of slanting sunshine, so she continued to stand there shaking her head until someone over yonder opened the roadway door and gestured with an upraised fist. She had forgotten the white cloth.

When she returned to the cell-room that unpleasant Hendrick-rider was baiting Alfred Cullin. "Did you tell 'em you'd sold out to the townfolks, Mister Cullin?"

The older, smaller man put a slow, icy stare upon the hard-eyed man. While staring at him Cullin addressed his employer. "Hendrick, I hope they hang you. If it warn't for you tryin' to bully the town an' hire a killer to back you up ... John: I'm glad my sister didn't live to see this day — you bastard!"

Frank let those words settle before asking Cullin a question. "Are you goin' back down yonder or are you goin' to stay in here?"

Cullin's answer was short and blunt. "Stayin' in here won't do a lick of good. I'm goin' back down to the barn."

12

The Last Day of Autumn Gold

TO the people in the jailhouse their world was localised. They had a dilemma that seemed unlikely to be resolved. Their collective mood was dour, except for the Hendrick-rider whose sneer was an added irritant. He had been so confident throughout that the others, including the other rangemen, had formed a solid dislike of the man.

Buffy busied herself cleaning up, trying to be cheerful, making excursions up front to scan as much as she could see from the recessed front window. Once, when the preacher joined her up there, between them they fired up the stove, made a fresh pot of coffee and while waiting for it to boil, stood like a pair of demoralised scarecrows, silent and pensive.

Eventually Buffy told the preacher they had to get Frank and the marshal out of there; find some place where they could be bathed and cared for that was clean — with fresh air.

Parson Ross glumly agreed without looking at her or speaking. When he had returned after resting and cleaning up he had been hopeful. As the hours passed and their dilemma got worse, his earlier mood of weary demoralisation returned.

Buffy went to the window, stood utterly still for a moment then spoke quietly. "Parson, there's something going on."

He joined her at the window. They glimpsed men moving in fits and starts between buildings across the way, in the back-alley. Buffy spoke. "What are they doing?"

Eli Ross speculated. Since those townsmen were passing southward, he made a guess. "They're goin' down by the blacksmith's shed, which'll put them opposite your barn. My guess is that they're goin' to brace the cowmen."

Buffy put a hand to her lips. "Mister Cullin said there was twenty-six, Parson."

Eli nodded as he watched the flitting shapes on the far side of town. "It may not be enough," he said.

They watched and waited. The men they saw for moments as they passed alone and together between the yonder buildings, seemed to be half the town, maybe two-thirds of the men around town.

Buffy went down into the cell-room to tell Frank and the marshal what she had seen. The stockmen listened too, even the hard-eyed man named Sam Owen. Now, he was no longer smiling.

Fred Baca would have got off his bunk but the pain was too much. It only arrived when he moved. He swore at his leg, groped for the pistol he had among the blankets and offered it to

Buffy. She shook her head and Frank wryly smiled at her without speaking.

When she returned to the office that mild-mannered rangeman said, "Mister Hendrick . . . ?"

"What!"

"However this ends if I was in your boots I'd sell out and go as far from the Heatherton country as I could ride."

Sam Owen snarled at the mild-mannered rider. "You likely would, Will, but we ain't all as yaller as you are."

What happened next took everyone's attention off what was happening outside. The mild-mannered cowboy called Will was standing near the rear of the cell beneath the window where fresh air came in. He was a nondescript individual, one of those men people saw every day and neither heeded nor remembered. He started forward, moving slowly. When he was close enough he smiled at the large man named Owen. "Sam, you're a four-flushin' son of a bitch. Maybe

Mister Hendrick don't think so but us fellers who had to ride with you think so."

Without warning the smaller man swung. Owen was probably too surprised at being attacked by a man he considered a nonentity. He did not raise his arms in time. The blow rattled his teeth when it slammed into his jaw.

Hendrick started to squawk. Frank shoved his scattergun through the steel straps and told Hendrick to shut up and stay out of it.

Owen was large and powerful. His adversary was muscular but no more than medium height, maybe even a tad shorter, but when he fought it occurred to Frank that, knowing he was at a disadvantage in brawls, once he attacked he did not stop. Whether he knew it or not, that was a small man's only reasonable tactic; make larger men defend themselves, which is exactly what the mild-mannered man did; he followed up his first jarring strike without allowing Sam Owen time to recover.

The cell was too small for the large man to get clear, which was another thing in the smaller man's favour. Every step Owen took backwards or sideward, the other rangeman countered as he repeatedly struck Sam Owen.

Owen desperately rallied. When he would have come forward the man called Will kicked a three-legged stool in Owen's way. The big man did not fall but he had to sidestep where Will was waiting.

Frank winced when Will caught Sam Owen over the heart with a powerful strike. Owen's knees loosened. Will hit him in the soft parts. When Owen doubled over to protect his middle, Frank and Fred Baca watched in fascination as Will answered a question they had begun to wonder about.

When Owen leaned, Will set himself directly in front and fired from the waist. Owen's hat flew, his head snapped, his eyes glazed. He fell like a tree. There was flung-back blood on his cheek.

Not a sound was made for several seconds. Baca softly said, "Now overhaul that old son of a bitch you work for," to the cowboy, who had his back to Baca's cell.

He acted as though he had not heard; walked to the front of the cell with his back to the unconscious man on the floor and John Hendrick, considered the other pair of rangemen across the little corridor and said, "You satisfied?"

They nodded. The man with the prominent Adam's-apple even grinned. "I wondered how long you was goin' to take the insults he give you, Will."

Baca growled at John Hendrick. "Pick him up, put him on the bunk. *Move, you old bastard!*"

Hendrick arose but was interrupted by the arrival of Parson Ross. He had missed the fight but the way Buffy was standing, stiff as a ramrod, eyes round with shock, he guessed the fight had upset her, and he was right, but he had returned to the cell-room to say about half of the townsmen were down in front of the livery barn calling for the stockmen to come out.

Frank asked if they had come out.

Eli nodded. "Six or eight of them. I'd guess the rest are inside the barn." Ross was apprehensive. "It'll be a massacre if shooting starts."

Frank looked at the marshal, who looked back. Baca knew about stand-offs. "If half the townfellers is out front, where are the other hall?"

Eli shrugged. He had no idea, but Fred Baca did. He said, "That stocky feller with the beard an' that ol' beanpole friend of his didn't impress me as havin' come down in the last rain."

It was a good evaluation. Jess Ames the stager and Wes Hamilton the harness-maker had crossed Front Street at the farther north end of town with most of the armed townsmen. They had walked the full distance southward with only one interruption, which occurred when they were passing a dilapidated old fence and a pony-sized brindle dog came through snarling, every hair on his back standing straight up.

The townsmen knew the old man who owned the dog as well as the dog. Jess Ames started walking directly toward the dog, arms away from his sides. He snarled as he moved. The big dog back-peddled which was the way he did when preparing to attack. The stager jumped on him, hurled his hat which struck the dog in the face, diverting him so the stager could get close enough to kick the big dog squarely in the rear hard enough to lift him off the ground.

The dog fled back through the old fence whining like a baby.

The southward march was resumed. Out front the townsmen were palavering with the delegation of stockmen. The men inside the barn were listening intently when Hamilton and Ames stopped their approach to listen. The beanpole nodded.

There was nothing sly nor strategic about the way the townsmen entered the barn — forty-one armed men cocking weapons as they proceeded up the runway.

Alfred Cullin, up front listening to the men in the roadway, turned slowly. So did the other men in the barn. What they saw was a mob which filled the runway from side to side; every man with a cocked rifle, carbine, six-gun or shotgun.

The townsmen halted, took individual aim at the stiff-standing rangemen with no one making a sound until the stager growled, "Put the guns down or use them. *Now!*"

The surprise had been too stunning. Alfred Cullin up front tossed his six-gun down. The men inside the barn did the same, some obeying sooner, some later, but they all disarmed themselves.

Cullin called to the men in the roadway. They came into the barn with townsmen behind them. No one had to tell them, they shucked their weapons and one lanky cowboy softly and disgustedly said, "Son of a bitch!"

Alfred Cullin walked to the bench, sat down and watched the others. The stockmen were waiting too. The harness-maker relaxed hip-shot, mostly relieved but still wary. Jess Ames growled for anyone with a belly-gun to throw it away. A portly, greying man replied irritably. "We don't use hide-outs, you old goat."

Ames, a short-tempered man, not tall but broad and powerful, holstered his Colt walked over and hit the portly rancher in the stomach. The portly man dropped to his knees. The stager looked around. "You sons of bitches get on your horses an' don't even look back until you're home. Saddle up — *now!*"

That disgusted lanky man went to a stall, led his animal out, shook his head and muttered under his breath. The other rangemen went after their animals, most of which were in the outside corrals. Townsmen followed and watched, guns cocked. Nothing more was said until the stockmen, were ready to ride, when two riders helped the injured portly cowman rig out. As they were doing this that lanky man faced the stager. "What about the fellers at the jailhouse?"

Before the short-tempered man could reply the harness-maker took it upon himself to make a decision. "Fetch their animals up to the jailhouse. You can have 'em. All but Mister Hendrick."

The lanky man glowered. "Why not him?"

The stager glared. "We're about half a mind to hang the son of a bitch ... You too if you get troublesome."

The lanky man led his horse up through the runway with the other stockmen following. Jess Ames called to the lanky man, who stopped and turned. Ames strolled closer as he spoke. "It's up to Mister Cullin. We'll hang Hendrick if he says so. The old bastard deserves it. He caused all this.

Go on up an' wait for us."

The lanky man hesitated, but the stager's fighting glance did not waver. A nearby rangeman said, "Leave it be, Ben."

The rangemen led their horses away with townsmen following. In front of the jailhouse everyone halted, the townsmen across the road in front of Lewis's store, guns ready.

Alfred Cullin got off his bench. He addressed the stager. "I'll take care of Hendrick. Except for the memory of my sister who was his wife, I'd help you hang him . . . I'll take care of him."

The stager nodded. As Cullin led his horse out of the barn more townsmen trailed after him. They joined the mob over in front of the store while Al Cullin handed his reins to the sullen-looking rangeman, rapped on the jailhouse door and when he was admitted he barely glanced at Parson Ross who had opened the door. He went down into the cell-room, told Frank and the marshal what had happened, and waited. Frank looked at Fred Baca, who rolled his eyes and nodded. "Key to them cells is up front in a drawer ... Mister Cullin, I'd like to keep Mister Hendrick and that mouthy rider of his."

Cullin shook his head. "They go too. Don't worry about Hendrick, I'll break him to lead."

Baca shrugged. Buffy went after the keys. None of the soiled, unshaven demoralised stockmen made a sound until their cells were opened, then the mild-mannered Hendrick-rider addressed Baca and Frank as the man he had whipped shuffled into the corridor. "You're welcome to this country," he said, and punched his former adversary in the back to get him untracked.

Cullin followed them leaving only four people where before there had been nearly twice that many. Buffy went up front to close up after the stockmen left. Parson Ross found a stool and sat on it.

Fred Baca was vigorously scratching

his leg; quite a bit of the swelling had gone down, there was less pain and more itch. He looked over at Frank. "You look like hell except your face is clean . . . This place stinks."

Frank smiled. "You're the marshal, it's your pig-pen."

Buffy returned with a light, firm step. She stopped in the cell opening, looked at the three men and made her pronouncement. "Parson, round up some men to help get these two down to my house behind the barn."

All three looked blankly at her.

"Frank and the marshal need baths. They need their bandages changed. I've got two empty rooms for them. I'll get Alicia to help me. You can come later and see to their mending . . . Parson?"

Eli Ross got off his stool and wordlessly left the cell. Fred Baca was staring at the livery-lady. "I don't need no dang nurse," he told her, and got a sharp retort. "You never needed one more — and from now on watch your language around womenfolk. You are filthy. I'll clean both of you up an — "

Baca reddened. "Clean us up . . . ?"

"A hot bath for the both of you with soap, clean clothes then — "

The marshal interrupted. "You don't give me no bath, lady. Not on your life!"

"All right, Marshal, Alicia can. She's more near your age if that's what's bothering you."

"Who is Alicia?"

"She's the local seamstress. Alicia Hovencroft. She — "

"Lady, I can't bend this leg an' I don't think soap an' hot water would be good for it . . . I'll take my own bath when I can."

Buffy saw Frank faintly grinning and turned on him. "You have objections too, Mister Zurdo?"

"Frank," he told her. "Nobody's goin' to give me an all-over bath who calls me Mister Zurdo."

"How about Frank, then?"

His faint grin lingered. "I got a scratch across the back. That don't call for no all-over bath."

Buffy's gaze was unrelenting. She regarded them both for a moment before speaking again. "All right. I'll get some cloth from Mister Lewis."

Both men looked blank.

"To make diapers with. You can be bathed wearing them."

The beanpole and the stager, plus a pair of brawny younger men arrived being herded along by Parson Ross. All but the preacher had six-guns, either in holsters or stuck in the front of their britches.

Without a word they entered the cell, lifted both wounded men on the straw-filled mattresses they were on, grunted and grumbled up the narrow corridor to the office and out the roadway door into the heat of a dying autumn day.

Onlookers stopped to stare as Buffy and the preacher led the way. Up at his watering hole Henry Bolton went inside, returned with a bottle, handed it to a youngster with orders to take it down yonder and give it to the livery-lady. He said to explain to her that whiskey was a medicinal, no matter what that Bible-banger said. He might have also said that it was a fair disinfectant when there was nothing else.

Buffy Devon's house was actually a cottage across the back alley from her barn. It stood between her largest corral and her buggy shed. When the wounded men were put in their rooms and she got rid of the men who had carried them down there, the youngster appeared, handed her the bottle and fled.

She asked Parson Ross if he'd stop by the sewing shop and ask if Alicia would come down to lend Buffy a hand. Eli departed on his errand as Buffy went into the kitchen to boil water. She was tired, dirty and hungry.

When Alicia arrived she told her what the problem was then took her into the rooms of her guests and introduced her.

Frank nodded pleasantly. Fred Baca's eyes steadily widened, as the women were leaving he beckoned Buffy back and whispered to her. "You said she was old as I am."

"I said, Marshal, she was near your age. That means give or take six, seven years."

"Well, but I figured she'd be real old and — "

Buffy straightened up in the doorway. "I'll get the cloth for your diapers," she said and walked away.

Baca called. "Frank?"

Zurdo answered from the adjoining room, "Yeah."

"Did you see that sewing-lady?"

"Yes."

"Well hell, she's pretty an' — "

"Buffy said she'd put diapers on us."

"*She'll* put 'em on us? Not on your damned life."

"Marshal, you got to be feelin' better."

"I could be dyin' an' I'd never let

no woman put diapers on me. If I got to wear 'em I'll put 'em on myself."

Frank had a question for the marshal. "How'd your mother handle it?"

"That don't have a damned thing to do with it. I was a baby then."

"You're actin' like one now, Marshal."

"You're goin' to let that girl put diapers on you?"

Frank's reply was slow in coming. "I'm in no position to put up a fight an' neither are you, so just relax. If it bothers you too much — close your eyes."

The women did not return until it was lamp-lighting time. Buffy had cleaned up, eaten, and was freshly dressed when they appeared with two trays — and a tiny jolt glass on each tray.

Alicia went into the marshal's room, Buffy went to feed Frank. He wanted to sit up but she put a firm hand on his chest and pressed. She smiled. "You want the whiskey first or the food?"

He wanted the food so she settled on

the edge of the bed to spoon feed him. When she finished she continued to sit there. She was very pretty, scrubbed and with her hair tidied up and all. As she arose she said, "You'll get your bath after breakfast in the morning." She cocked her head a little. "I got the cotton for the diapers from Mister Lewis."

Frank's back began to itch. He could not scratch it so he gritted his teeth. An uninvited thought arrived to make him smile as shadows settled. Fred Baca was going to buck like a bay steer after breakfast tomorrow, injured leg or not.

Frank hadn't fallen to sleep in a long time smiling. He did this particular night. Once, he awakened. The night had turned cold. Indian summers never lasted; they were actually autumn's good-bye, winter would follow — and snow.

So much for getting to warm country before winter. Well hell, a man's life from the time he was calved was one damned trade-off after another. This time along with the danged snow he got a pretty blue-eyed woman. This time the trade-off wasn't so bad.

THE END

Other titles in the Linford Western Library:

TOP HAND
Wade Everett

The Broken T was big. But no ranch is big enough to let a man hide from himself.

GUN WOLVES OF LOBO BASIN
Lee Floren

The Feud was a blood debt. When Smoke Talbot found the outlaws who gunned down his folks he aimed to nail their hide to the barn door.

SHOTGUN SHARKEY
Marshall Grover

The westbound coach carrying the indomitable Larry and Stretch headed for a shooting showdown.

FIGHTING RAMROD
Charles N. Heckelmann

Most men would have cut their losses, but Frazer counted the bullets in his guns and said he'd soak the range in blood before he'd give up another inch of what was his.

LONE GUN
Eric Allen

Smoke Blackbird had been away too long. The Lequires had seized the Blackbird farm, forcing the Indians and settlers off, and no one seemed willing to fight! He had to fight alone.

THE THIRD RIDER
Barry Cord

Mel Rawlins wasn't going to let anything stand in his way. His father was murdered, his two brothers gone. Now Mel rode for vengeance.